D1084136

SETTLED OUT OF COURT

In spite of its title this story by the author of *Brothers in Law* includes his usual cheerful tour of the Courts. It opens with the conviction for murder upon entirely perjured evidence of a wealthy financier who has the unusual characteristic of never telling lies.

HENRY CECIL

Settled out of Court

London
MICHAEL JOSEPH

First published by
MICHAEL JOSEPH LTD
26 *Bloomsbury Street*
*London, W.C.*1
1959

© *copyright Henry Cecil 1958, 1959*

Set and printed in Great Britain by Tonbridge Printers Ltd,
Peach Hall Works, Tonbridge, Kent, in Baskerville eleven on
twelve point, on paper made by Henry Bruce at Currie,
Midlothian, and bound by James Burn at Esher, Surrey

CONTENTS

CHAPTER ONE

Nothing like the Truth

'TAKE it easy,' said the warder, who led Lonsdale Walsh down the stairs from the dock in Court 1 of the Old Bailey, 'you can always appeal.'

The warder was a kindly man and realised that the prisoner was upset. He was not altogether surprised. A lot of prisoners became upset, even when they were convicted of lesser crimes than murder. Some of them shouted, some of them cried, some of them collapsed. Lonsdale Walsh did none of these things. He simply went very red in the face, very, very red. The warder rightly assumed from this that Lonsdale Walsh disagreed with the verdict of the jury, and he was preparing to add a few further words of advice about appealing. Not because he thought that an appeal would be likely to succeed, but simply out of kindness, to give the man some hope.

The warder had not been surprised that Lonsdale Walsh took the verdict badly, but he was most surprised and pained by the answer to his kindly advice. The convicted man was a very wealthy financier and, apart from the unfortunate matter of the murder, had never been in the hands of the police. Some prisoners have two warders to accompany them down the stairs, some even three. One should surely be enough for an otherwise respectable financier; but he was not. Lonsdale Walsh's answer was to turn round and knock out the warder with a well-aimed blow to the chin. Having thus relieved his feelings to a small extent, he then waited quietly for the inevitable to

7

happen. But there was not much they could do to him. You can't add anything useful to imprisonment for life.

Later, Lonsdale Walsh arranged for £200 to be sent to the warder, with the result that that kindly man remarked to his wife that he wouldn't mind being knocked out again at the same price, preferably just before they took their holiday. It will be realised from this payment that Lonsdale Walsh had no grievance against the warder. He had simply been compelled to lash out at someone, and the warder was nearest to hand.

It must be very unpleasant to be convicted of murder and even more unpleasant to be so convicted on perjured evidence. Any reasonable man would resent this. But there was a special reason why it was worse for Lonsdale Walsh than for anyone else. He was allergic to lies. Just as some people break out into a rash if they come near a cat or a strawberry, so a deliberate untruth had from his childhood revolted him. It was not a question of morality or religion at all. His devotion to the truth was like a purely physical complaint. No doubt he himself would have told a lie to save his own life or the life of someone for whom he had a sufficient regard or to save his country, but he had never been put in the position of having to do any of these things. He had told no lies at his trial, not even to his own solicitors and counsel. And the evidence against him was almost entirely perjured from beginning to end. With the possible exception of their names and addresses nearly everything stated by the chief witnesses against him had been untrue.

If this would be difficult for an ordinary person to bear, it was impossible for Lonsdale Walsh. And so the warder got his £200. Take it easy indeed!

Lonsdale Walsh was the child of well-to-do middle-class parents. They were very ordinary, decent people and, except to the extent that no one is absolutely normal, they were without 'isms' or allergies of any kind. Nor, curiously enough, did they notice anything wrong with Lonsdale until it was pointed out to them. But one day they were a little surprised to be asked by Lonsdale's headmaster to come to see him. They wondered whether the discussion was to be about the boy's career or whether he had got into trouble of some kind. They were not unduly alarmed. Lonsdale was a big boy for his age and good with his fists. But they could not think that he would be guilty of anything worse than a schoolboy prank. So perhaps it was his career after all. But, then, why ask them in the middle of term? Perhaps he had been bullying smaller (or even larger) boys. They knew that he was very determined to get his own way but, as he never told lies to his parents and never tried to knock them down, they could not imagine that he had done anything terrible. On the way to the school they discussed every possibility they could think of, but they were still somewhat mystified by the time they were shown into the headmaster's study.

'Nice of you to come,' he said. 'So sorry to have to trouble you, but we're a little worried about Lonsdale.'

The parents were relieved. This couldn't be anything very bad. You can't be 'a little worried' about a boy whom you're going to expel.

'Oh?' said Lonsdale's father.

'I thought you might be able to help us,' went on the headmaster.

'What's the trouble?'

'Well,' said the headmaster, 'you must know all about it, but it is becoming a bit embarrassing.'

'Embarrassing? I'm afraid I really don't know what you're talking about.'

'I'm sorry,' said the headmaster. 'It's this truth business, you know. It's really getting us down a bit.'

'Truth business?' said Lonsdale's father. 'I haven't the

faintest idea what you're talking about. Has he been telling lies or something? It's not like him.'

'Lies?' said the headmaster, 'indeed no. I'm afraid I wish he would sometimes.'

'Look, headmaster,' said Mr Walsh, 'my wife and I are simple people, but I hope I may say of average intelligence. Would you kindly explain in plain intelligible language what your complaint is about our boy?'

'It's not exactly a complaint,' said the headmaster uncomfortably, 'but, to put it bluntly, we think he ought to see a psychiatrist.'

'Who's we?'

'His form master, his housemaster and I.'

'Why on earth should he see a psychiatrist? He's a normal enough boy. He works well, doesn't he? He's good at games. Bit of a bully, perhaps, but that you can easily cope with at a school like this.'

'What you say is quite right, Mr Walsh,' said the headmaster. 'It's quite true that he is inclined to fight his way through, if he wants anything badly enough but, as you say, we're quite used to dealing with that sort of thing here. No, it's something much more unusual. Indeed, it's unique in my experience. But I can't imagine that you don't know all about it.'

'Well, I'm afraid we don't,' said Lonsdale's father. 'Will you be good enough to enlighten us?'

'Well, anyway,' said the headmaster, 'you must have noticed that he always tells the truth.'

'Really!' said Mr Walsh. 'I'm a very busy man and it's quite a long journey here. You haven't asked us to come and see you just because we've tried to bring our boy up decently.'

'Please don't be annoyed,' said the headmaster, 'I assure you that I have only the boy's interests at heart—and yours too, of course.'

'I'm sorry,' said Mr Walsh, 'please forgive me. But my

wife and I would really like to know what you are driving at.'

'Well, as you don't seem to know,' said the headmaster, 'I'd better start from the beginning. Now naturally we like boys to tell the truth. But, of course, the normal boy doesn't always do so. Usually it's to avoid unpleasant consequences for himself or someone else. But occasionally it's simply out of kindness. Just as we don't hurt people's feelings by saying what we really think of them.'

'You find that Lonsdale speaks his mind too freely, is that it?'

'He certainly does, but that isn't it by a long way. Not only does he invariably say exactly what he thinks, not only does he invariably tell the truth, however unpleasant the consequences for himself or anyone else, but, if he knows that anyone else is telling a lie, he . . . he . . . well I know it may sound ridiculous to you, as you don't seem to have noticed it at home—so let me say something else first. As I've said, we like boys to tell the truth, but equally, or perhaps even more important, we don't encourage sneaks.'

'You're not suggesting——' began Mr Walsh indignantly, but the headmaster held up his hand.

'Please let me finish,' he said. 'I am quite satisfied that your boy is not a deliberate sneak—that is to say, he never deliberately tells tales about other boys. I'm sure it's not deliberate.'

'What isn't deliberate?'

'Well, every time Lonsdale knows that someone is telling a lie he—he goes red in the face, red like a turkey cock. In other words, if the truth is in question and Lonsdale knows it, the master has only to look at him to find the answer. I repeat, I'm quite sure the boy can't help it. He's got an allergy. Lies make him nearly burst. It isn't healthy, Mr Walsh. It doesn't so much matter here, but I'm thinking of his later career. Of course, truth is very important. We all realise that. And I must congratulate you on Lonsdale's truthfulness. But—but—now I'm not a psychiatrist, but, in my view, if he goes on like this without any assistance, if he goes into the world with this allergy, a world which unfortunately abounds with lies, he may very well find himself in a mental home. If you had seen the look on that boy's face sometimes when he knew the truth was not being told, you would understand why I am warning you. Now, of course, he may adapt himself to the behaviour of the world, I may have sent for you unnecessarily, but, in my view, I should be failing in my duty as his headmaster if I did not say that, in my opinion, your boy ought to be seen by a psychiatrist as soon as possible.'

Mr and Mrs Walsh said nothing for a moment. They simply looked at each other. Then Mr Walsh said:

'I must confess we've never noticed anything very peculiar. Now I come to think of it, the boy is very outspoken. But I've always liked that, and rather encouraged it. Are you sure it's more than that?'

'If you will treat the conversation as entirely confidential, then I'll send for the boy and ask him a question.'

'Certainly,' said Lonsdale's parents.

Lonsdale soon arrived and greeted his parents in the normal way. 'Tell me, Walsh,' said the headmaster to Lonsdale, 'what do you honestly think of Mr Thompson?'

'Bloody awful, sir,' said Lonsdale.

'There's no need to swear,' said his father.

'The headmaster asked me what I honestly thought,' said the boy. 'That was the only way I could express it honestly.'

'This Mr Thompson,' said Mr Walsh to the headmaster, 'what is your opinion of him? In confidence, of course.'

The headmaster coughed.

'He's a very good man,' he said eventually.

Lonsdale blushed furiously.

'May I go now please, sir?' he asked.

A month later Lonsdale was interviewed by an eminent psychiatrist, Dr Harvey McLong.

'Well, how's school?' began Dr McLong.

'All right,' said Lonsdale.

'I see,' said Dr McLong. 'Nothing more than that? Just all right?'

'Yes,' said Lonsdale, 'it's all right.'

'And what's it like at home?'

'All right,' said Lonsdale.

'No better than at school?' asked Dr McLong.

'It's different,' said Lonsdale.

'I see,' said Dr McLong, and there was a pause. 'I gather,' he went on, 'that you're happy both at home and at school?'

'Yes,' said Lonsdale.

'Nothing the matter?'

'Not that I can think of.'

'Why d'you think you've come to see me?'

'Because I'm growing up, I suppose, and you're going to tell me things.'

'I see,' said Dr McLong, and there was another pause. Then he decided he must get nearer the subject.

'Do you always tell the truth, Lonsdale?'

'As far as I know, I do.'

'Why?'

'Because I do.'

'Is there no other reason? Isn't it because you want to be trusted?'

'I've never thought.'

'D'you know the story of Cassandra, the Trojan prophetess, who had a curse laid on her that she should always prophesy the truth and never be believed?'

'That's a horrible story,' said Lonsdale, and went very red in the face.

'A thing like that upsets you?'

'Yes, it does.'

'Why?'

'How should I know? I don't like it, that's all.'

'You like the truth, don't you?'

'How d'you mean, like it?'

'Well, you always tell the truth yourself and you like other people to do so too.'

'I suppose so.'

'Why?'

'I don't know. I just do. Same as I like stewed apricots and not stewed prunes.'

'Good,' said Dr McLong. 'You've never thought of joining our profession, have you?'

'No,' said Lonsdale.

'Why not?'

'Because I think it's a lot of . . .' and Lonsdale then said a word which was seldom used in Dr McLong's consulting-room, except by men friends who happened to be calling on him for a chat, and a few women patients who wanted to show off.

'People used to make that sort of remark about a lot of things which have since proved to be very useful. We're a fairly new profession. You must be indulgent with us.'

Lonsdale said nothing.

'When I mentioned the story of Cassandra to you, you went very red in the face. Did you feel anything?'

'I felt hot.'

'Why?'

'Because I didn't like the story.'

'But you don't feel hot when you see stewed prunes, do you?'

'No.'

'Or when you see someone you don't like?'

'I suppose not.'

'Then why at the story of Cassandra?'

'Because I do.'

'And you feel the same if you hear anyone tell lies, don't you?'

'Yes.'

'Why?'

'Because I do.'

'It isn't really an answer to say that. We don't eat because we eat. We eat because we're hungry. That's right, isn't it?'

'I suppose so.'

'Then why d'you feel hot when somebody tells lies?'

'Because I don't like it, I suppose.'

'But you don't feel hot at everything you don't like?'

'No.'

'Then why at lies?'

'I don't know. I just do.'

'But you must realise that in a civilised society lies have to be told. Sometimes you have to lie to be kind to a person. If a girl asks you whether you like her dress, it wouldn't be kind to say you didn't, would it?'

'No.'

'Don't you want to be kind to people?'

'Sometimes.'

'Which would you prefer, to tell the truth and hurt someone's feelings or to tell a lie to avoid hurting them?'

'To tell the truth.'

'But that wouldn't be kind.'

'I didn't say it would.'

'What is your object in life?'

'To be a millionaire.'

'Why?'

'Because, if you're a millionaire, you can do lots of things.'

'What sort of things?'

'Oh—I don't know, have swimming pools and yachts and things.'

'And girls all round the place?'

Lonsdale said nothing.

'Well, what are you thinking about?' asked Dr McLong.

'I thought you'd have got there before.'

'To girls, you mean? You thought you'd come here to talk about girls?'

'Yes.'

'Are you disappointed that we haven't talked about them?'

'No.'

'Why not?'

'Plenty of time for them later, when I grow up.'

'What d'you like talking about?'

'Depends who I'm talking to.'

'What would you like to talk to me about?'

'Nothing.'

'I see,' said Dr McLong. 'You're not exactly co-operative.'

'What's that?'

'You're not trying to help me.'

'Help you do what?'

'Help you.'

'I don't want any help.'

'I think you do. D'you want to go through life getting red in the face every time someone tells a lie?'

'I don't mind.'

'You will.'

But it was many years before Dr McLong was proved right. Until his conviction for murder, Lonsdale was not personally affected by his complaint. Indeed, to a considerable extent, it stood him in good stead. During his career it became known by everyone with whom he had dealings that, though he would use every effort to get his own way, the lie was the one weapon he would not use. 'Walsh's word' became a synonym for the truth.

It was the other people who suffered, not he. He would not tolerate lies in any circumstances. Once, an office boy in a company of his started to take money out of the petty cash to put on horses. Eventually he had a lucky win and paid it all back. By a miscalculation, however, he paid back rather too much and his offences were discovered. His immediate superior, however, was so impressed at the boy's honesty in repaying the money that he tried to hush it up and told a lie about it. When this was discovered, Lonsdale immediately ordered the dismissal of the man who had covered the crimes of the office boy. The latter was allowed to remain.

Lonsdale's allergy only related to the spoken or written lie. Mere dishonesty was a totally different matter. He had no particular objection to the burglar, even if he used violence. But the woman who lied to the customs authorities in order to smuggle in some trifles provoked him to fury. He could have sympathy with a man who murdered his wife, but none with a man who tricked a woman into bigamy by pretending he was single. He never considered whether he over-valued truth at the expense of other qualities, any more than the average sufferer from one disease seriously considers whether he would prefer to have another.

CHAPTER TWO

Discovery and Conviction

Lonsdale Walsh started his career as an accountant and he soon became deeply interested in finance. His parents left him a little capital and by careful, speculative investment he quickly increased it. By the time he was forty he was of importance in the City. By the time he was fifty he was a very wealthy man, and by the time he was convicted of murder, at the age of fifty-five, he was pretty well a millionaire.

His conviction arose as a direct result of the battles which often take place between financiers. Sometimes the contestants are on the same board, and it was so in this case. A great struggle was taking place for the control of the Anglo-Saxon Development Corporation Limited. This company had been nurtured by Lonsdale Walsh almost from its birth, and it had become one of the biggest and wealthiest companies in the country. Lonsdale was determined to retain control of it, but he had an equally determined opponent in Adolphus Barnwell or, more accurately, in Adolphus Barnwell's wife.

Jo Barnwell had been a singularly attractive girl and at forty-five she was as attractive a woman as Lonsdale knew. But there was no doubt at all that it was she who kept Adolphus at it. Probably he would have preferred to retire into the country and farm. But that sort of life was not for Jo. She liked to be at the centre of things. She enjoyed a fight. But though she did not lead her regiment from behind and would have been the first to admit her influence over her husband, she preferred to win her battles through him. So she never personally went on the board of any of Adolphus' companies. She contented herself with telling him what to do when he was on them. He gladly accepted her advice for two reasons. It was good advice and it made things easier at home. Once or twice in their early days he had made a mild protest at some of Jo's more outrageous suggestions, but she quickly put him in his place, and it must be said that, until he was murdered, he was very happy there.

Jo and Lonsdale often met and they each enjoyed those occasions. It was the attraction of opposites. Jo would tell a lie as soon as look at you, if it would serve her purpose, but she was highly intelligent and realised that, if you want to make the best use of the lie as a weapon, it should not be used too often. And it must be a good one. She was the one person whose lies had a fascination for Lonsdale. He loathed them instinctively but in her case they had the attraction which repulsive-looking objects have for some people. He would even try to provoke one on occasion, much as a person sometimes squeezes a painful sore to make it hurt more. No one is quite sure whether that is done because of the relief when the pressure stops, or whether there is something masochistic about it. Whatever the reason, Lonsdale enjoyed meeting Jo, and they danced many times together, while Adolphus sat quite happily in the background.

Lonsdale's wife had died young, and he had never remarried. But his relationship with Jo was completely blameless on the surface. Most of the time they fought and in their words and actions towards each other there was never the slightest hint of the affection which may well have existed under the surface. Apart altogether from their verbal battles which were little, if anything, more than play, they fought in earnest behind the scenes.

Had the opportunity arisen, each would cheerfully have made the other bankrupt. They asked each other for no quarter, and never gave it. The only difference between them was that Jo knew that she could always take Lonsdale's word, while he knew that he could never accept anything she said with any degree of assurance, unless it was on a matter of no importance to her.

The battle for the control of the Anglo-Saxon Corporation had only been in progress for a short time when the events, which were to place Lonsdale in the dock, started to take shape. In the course of gathering his forces together for the main attack, Lonsdale had exchanged a number of important and highly confidential letters with some of his associates. Knowledge of their contents would have been of the greatest possible value to the Barnwell forces. Jo indeed considered the idea of a burglary, but rejected it as too dangerous and too doubtful of success. She was quite right to reject the idea. Lonsdale had taken sufficient precautions to deal with that possibility. He kept all such correspondence at his bank. So Jo had to think again.

One day Lonsdale received a letter from the Barnwell solicitors informing him that their client, Adolphus Barnwell, was proposing to bring an action for slander against him, and asking for the names of solicitors who would accept service on his behalf of such proceedings. The nature and occasion of the slander were mentioned, and Lonsdale knew that it was a pure invention. He was not unduly worried, although he had a vague feeling that there was more behind the threat than he could see. He went straight to his solicitors, Messrs Slograve, Plumb & Co., and interviewed Mr Slograve.

'What's this all about?' he asked.

'Did you say what the letter alleges?'

'Certainly not. I didn't even discuss the matter. What's behind it?'

'Let me think,' said Mr Slograve. After a moment or

two, he said: 'I'm afraid I think I know what they're after. You're not going to be pleased.'

'What is it?'

'The Annual General of the Anglo-Saxon is in about nine months, isn't it?'

'Yes. But what's that got to do with it?' Lonsdale was becoming a little apprehensive.

'This slander action will be so framed that the correspondence we all know about and which Barnwell would dearly love to see before the Annual General, will be material to the action.'

'And?'

'Accordingly you will have to disclose it to them.'

'I'll do nothing of the kind.'

'I'm afraid you'll have to. You'll have to swear an affidavit saying what documents are in your or your agent's possession.'

'We'll destroy them.'

'Then you'll not only to have to admit that fact but they can ask you what was in them.'

'My God!' said Lonsdale. 'It's that bloody woman. What can I do about it?'

'I really don't know,' said Mr Slograve. 'We could try to drag things out, but we'd never succeed in avoiding discovery before the meeting.'

'But the whole action's a fraud. It's just brought to get a sight of the correspondence.'

'I know. The more I think of it, the plainer it becomes.'

'But surely you can prevent a thing like that? It's an abuse of the process of the Court. Isn't that what you'd call it?'

'Certainly it is. But how can we prove it? All they have to do is to call their witness to say you said what's alleged.'

'But it'll be rank perjury.'

'But how can you show it to be? There's only your word against his.'

'It's an outrage,' said Lonsdale. 'Surely the law is strong enough to deal with a situation like this.'

'I'm afraid not,' said Mr Slograve. 'Of course, we'll go to counsel about it, to see if we can avoid disclosing the letters, but, as the whole object of the action is to look at them, I can't conceive that they won't frame their allegations so as to make any case for refusing to disclose them untenable.'

'So that anyone, who's unscrupulous enough, can just invent an allegation in order to look at someone else's private documents?'

'I'm afraid that is so, provided it's skilfully done and provided at least one person is prepared to commit perjury. Of course, we can fight them all the way, but in my view we shall lose and, however much we appeal, we'll never keep the fight going beyond the meeting. We can only hope that Mr Barnwell has a coronary thrombosis before discovery.'

'What good would that do? That woman would carry on after him.'

'Well, she couldn't, as a matter of fact. A slander action dies when the plaintiff dies.'

'I thought the executors could carry on with an action started by a man who dies?'

'That rule doesn't apply to libel or slander actions. I don't pretend to be a great lawyer, but that's one of the things you can take from me.'

It was not long after this conversation that Adolphus Barnwell died, not from coronary thrombosis—but suddenly and violently. That was the end of the slander action, but not of Jo Barnwell. And, three months after her husband died, she saw to it that Lonsdale stood in the dock charged with the murder. And the jury said 'Guilty,' and the judge said 'Imprisonment for life.'

CHAPTER THREE

Spikey Lee's Chance

For the first few days after his conviction Lonsdale was hardly sane, but he pulled himself together sufficiently to sign his Notice of Appeal to the Court of Criminal Appeal. He was present when his appeal was dismissed. Once again he had to be forcibly restrained. He was led away shouting unintelligibly.

After a few days in the prison hospital he recovered sufficiently to take stock of his position. His counsel advised him that it was impossible to apply to the Attorney-General for leave to appeal to the House of Lords, as there were no grounds for making such an application. So Lonsdale petitioned the Home Secretary and wrote to his M.P. for help. All his attempts to have his case reviewed failed, and the governor of the prison eventually told him that it was useless for him to batter his head against a brick wall and that he would be well advised to accept his sentence with resignation.

'But there wasn't a word of truth in the evidence for the prosecution, sir.'

'I'm afraid a lot of convicted people say that. Now, you're an intelligent man. Your sentence will be reviewed in ten years and any time after that . . .'

'Ten years!' said Lonsdale. 'That makes it a bit early to be measured for my coming out suit.'

After a few months in prison, Lonsdale asked his only daughter, Angela, to visit him, and he was eventually allowed to see her.

'I want you to do something for me,' he said.

'Of course. What is it?'

'I want you to go round the Courts and find a barrister whom you consider to have intelligence of the highest class and to have a resilient mind. A chap who isn't hide-bound. A man who's prepared to consider new ideas or new situations, not just dismissing them because he's never come across them before. I don't mind if he's old or young, well-known or not, but he must have the qualities I've mentioned. He won't be easy to find, so go everywhere. Take your time. High Court, County Court, Sessions, Old Bailey, Magistrate's Court—but find me the right man.'

'Of course I will, father, but what . . .'

'Never mind the reason. Find him. Now there's something else I want you to do. To some extent you can do it at the same time. I want you to find a High Court judge with the same qualities, someone of the highest intelligence but who's still prepared to learn. Will you do it?'

'Well, of course, father, if it'll make you happier.'

'It will,' said Lonsdale, 'and, when you've made your selection, let me know their names and addresses.'

While Angela was making her tour of the Courts, her father was concentrating on the plan he had made. A person of his character must have something to live for, something in the not too distant future. By the time of his conversation with Angela, Lonsdale had completely recovered from the appalling shock of his conviction and the sense of utter frustration. At once his agile and deter-mined mind began to consider ways and means of attaining his object before it was too late to be worth while. Neither the decision of the Court of Criminal Appeal nor the rejection of his plea by the Home Secretary, nor the governor's advice had in the least altered his resolve, which was to have the jury's verdict in his case set aside and, incidentally, to show Jo Barnwell that it was not as easy as she must have thought to put Lonsdale Walsh in prison for life. He gave her full credit for what she had achieved. It required ingenuity and boldness, and, if it had not also entailed the use of the lie from start to finish, Lonsdale might even have admired her handiwork.

Day after day and night after night he pictured the scene of his triumph and of Jo's anger when, in spite of the apparently insuperable difficulties, he finally triumphed over her. But, though he allowed himself these dreams as a necessary entertainment during his drab prison life, he spent much time in working out, from the practical point of view, how he was going to attain his object.

His first step was to find a co-prisoner, due for release in a few months, whom he considered a suitable ally. He must be a man with many previous convictions, someone for whom crime was simply a means to an end and who had gone on too long in the business to become respectable, who indeed would consider himself a recidivist if he took an honest job. He must be a man who, as Becky Sharp might have been, would be honest on ten thousand a year. In other words, he must not be a man who enjoyed crime for its own sake and who needed the excitement involved. Such men are often exhibitionists and would be very dangerous to employ. Lonsdale needed a man for whom money and not notoriety was the spur. Eventually he chose Spikey Lee as someone who came nearest to his requirements. Spikey was a versatile criminal and was as prepared to go in for a long-firm fraud as to climb up a drainpipe and tie up the lady of the house with her husband's pyjama-cord, preparatory to ransacking the bedroom. On one occasion his calculations went wrong and the husband was there too, with the pyjama cord safely round him. He had also tried, not very successfully, a little forgery, and once (and he was heartily ashamed of this) a little blackmail.

'Honest, guv,' he said to Lonsdale (who was known in prison as 'The Guv'), 'honest, I wish I 'adn't. And that

ain't 'cos I got five years out of it. It's the only time I
meant it when I said I was sorry. The old basket didn't
believe me any more than 'e did the other times. But I
told 'im straight—"I'm sorry, my Lord," I said. "Straight
I am. It's a dirty game, and I swear I'll never do it again.
But the money seemed so easy," I said. "You see, my
Lord," I said, "I take a lot of risks when I go climbing up
a drainpipe. I may fall and break my blooming neck for
one thing. And I may get caught for another. And there
may not be anything worth taking in the end. And when I
saw this easy money—with no drainpipes, no house-
holders with rolling pins, nothing at all except to say
'more please' and out it comes all nice and easy, well I fell
for it, my Lord. And I'd like to say to Mr X and Mrs Y
and Miss Z that I'm really and truly sorry for what I done
to 'em, and if I still 'ad the money I'd give it back." I can't
say I really meant that bit, guv, but it just come out and it
didn't make no difference as I'd spent it all long before. "I
believe you're sorry," said the old basket—"you're sorry
because you were caught." "Well, that's true, my Lord,"
I said, "but I'm sorry for what I done too. I don't say I'll
go straight when I come out, but I'll never do that again."
"You won't get the chance for some time," he said. "Five
years." It was quite fair, guv. It's a real dirty game and I
don't 'old with it. Easy, though.'

And Lonsdale observed a look of regret on Spikey's face,
as he savoured in retrospect the ease of the living which
he had renounced.

It was not the renunciation which made Lonsdale
think that Spikey was his man, but his obvious desire for
ease. Here was the man who would work for money and
who would certainly not exchange it for his picture in the
Sunday newspapers and a pat on the back from the police.
In other words here was a man who could be completely
trusted so long as he was paid. And Lonsdale intended
that he should be paid.

The whole prison population knew who Lonsdale was and accordingly Spikey could believe his ears when Lonsdale mentioned what he was prepared to pay for Spikey's co-operation. To Spikey it was the fulfilment of his life's dream. Always to know where the next pint was coming from and without having to work for it. It was like winning a football pool. For Lonsdale had promised Spikey a substantial lump sum and an annuity. And, once again, Lonsdale had the reward of his passion for the truth. Spikey really believed that he meant it. Anticipation is often sweeter than realisation, and Spikey's last few weeks in prison were some of the most enjoyable he had ever spent in his life.

CHAPTER FOUR

A Tour of the Courts

Angela Walsh was a double First but she had the great advantage of looking and talking like a charming Third. She was as intelligent as her father, not quite so determined and with an unexaggerated regard for the truth. She was devoted to her father but she had told him the normal lies which normal children tell normal parents, with this qualification, that from a very early age she never told him an untruth without being quite certain that she would not be found out.

She was deeply distressed at her father's predicament and anxious to do all she could to help him. She had but the vaguest idea of what was behind his request, and she did not attempt to find out. She knew that she would learn in the end and she simply concentrated on the task which her father had given her. Had the circumstances not been so tragic, it would have been a most interesting assignment and, even as it was, she was able to get considerable interest and even amusement from her tour of the Courts. At the end of it she could have written a most entertaining little book containing sketches of judges, barristers, solicitors, witnesses and the other people who are involved in civil and criminal trials. It was a highly concentrated tour and, in the course of it, she reflected that it might be no bad thing if such a tour could be introduced into the curriculum of children about to leave school, or at any rate of university students. Although there would obviously be periods of boredom in such a course, it would for the most part, she thought from her own experiences, combine instruction with entertainment to such a high degree that even the dullest student must learn a good deal.

Although, in view of her father's wealth and previous position, she could easily have obtained introductions to solicitors or barristers to show her round, she thought it better, to begin with at any rate, to go entirely by herself. She did not want her own judgment to be affected by the views of lawyers of experience. She must make this choice by herself. Once a well-known lawyer had advised her on the subject, she would have difficulty in relying on her own inexperienced judgment. How could she tell whether the judgment of the lawyer was right? Only the barrister she was looking for could have given her the right advice.

So round the courts she went by herself. She heard impassioned pleas at the Old Bailey, dry legal arguments in the Chancery Division and incredible evidence by bankrupts, explaining how they had managed to dispose of certain untraceable assets, explanations which no one pretended to believe and which the bankrupts themselves sometimes put forward rather apologetically, as the best they could do at short notice. She heard husbands' and wives' stories of marital unhappiness, and motorists' protests at the diligence of the police in prosecuting them for obstruction while armed robbers remained loose, and so on. A little book! She could have written several volumes. Sometimes she could not resist waiting, although she knew that no one in the case was the man for her father. Very sensibly she felt that she must have some relaxation and she used such occasions for that purpose. And she would have been very sorry indeed to miss such incidents as the cross-examination of a witness by Mr Tewkesbury, that astonishing solicitor, who could give a tight-rope walker points in the way in which he managed to remain on the roll of solicitors.

Mr Tewkesbury's client was a lady of easy virtue. She chose to be defended instead of pleading guilty because she had come before a magistrate who was well known for his habit of exercising his powers under a very ancient Act of Parliament. These powers in effect enabled him to send prostitutes to prison, although the maximum fine for the offence with which they were charged was forty shillings. The method was to call upon them to find sureties for their good behaviour. In default of such sureties being found, the ancient Act entitled the Court to send them to prison. So Mr Tewkesbury was from time to time, when he was sober enough, pressed into service by these ladies. And excellent service he gave. Magistrates in the districts where such ladies abound have very full lists, and, if every one of them insisted on pleading not guilty, no magistrate would be able to get through his list. Moreover, the offences with which they were charged were not always easy to prove, as it required proof that at least one member of the public had been annoyed. As, normally, no member of the public is prepared to come and give evidence that he was annoyed, the witnesses in such cases almost invariably consist of policemen. Mr Tewkesbury knew that, by spinning out the case to the greatest possible length, he might eventually prevail on the magistrate to dismiss the charge, not simply to put an end to the ordeal but because, in the course of asking so many questions, it might well happen that some kind of doubt might emerge. The lady in question was entitled to the benefit of the doubt, and, after three-quarters of an hour of Mr Tewkesbury, a magistrate could not be blamed for being in doubt. Indeed, the endeavours to follow conscientiously all Mr Tewkesbury's questions and submissions sometimes made more than one magistrate doubt if he was fit for anything else that afternoon.

It is not always appreciated by members of the legal profession and the public that the conscientious judge is always listening, listening intently, even when his eyes are half-closed, and it is an extremely wearying ordeal to have to listen intently to arguments which vary in infinite variety between the intelligent and the unintelligible. Interruptions in an effort to make a point clear usually only succeed in making it even more obscure, and the business of sorting out the various arguments and trying to make some reasonable sense of them occasionally almost reduces the listener to tears. He does not actually cry, but his exhaustion is sometimes indicated by a sudden exasperated remark from a judge who is noted for his placidity.

Mr Tewkesbury's cross-examination during Angela's visit was directed to the policeman's evidence that a man had been annoyed by his client's solicitations.

MR TEWKESBURY: Now, officer, I want you to follow this next question very closely.

CONSTABLE: I try to follow all your questions closely.

TEWKESBURY: And with what measure of success?

MAGISTRATE: You needn't answer that question.

TEWKESBURY: But, sir, with the greatest possible respect, am I not entitled to an answer?

MAGISTRATE: No.

TEWKESBURY: But, sir, unless I know the measure of success which the officer has in following my questions, it becomes more difficult for me to frame the next question.

MAGISTRATE: So far you seem to have overcome your difficulties most manfully. I have observed no lack of questions.

TEWKESBURY: Your Worship's courtesy overwhelms me.

MAGISTRATE (*to himself*): I wish it would.

TEWKESBURY: Is it now convenient, sir, that I should resume my cross-examination where I left off?

MAGISTRATE: Very well.

TEWKESBURY: Well then, officer, would you be kind enough to tell me the measure of success with which you have understood my previous questions?

MAGISTRATE: I've just said he needn't answer that question.

TEWKESBURY: But, sir, did I not understand you to change your mind and say I may ask it? If I may say so, the greatest judges change their minds. *Judex mutabilis, judex amabilis*, if I may say so.

MAGISTRATE: Mr Tewkesbury, would you kindly continue your cross-examination of this witness. I've fifty summonses to hear after this.

TEWKESBURY: I don't know how your Worship does it and retains your good humour.

MAGISTRATE (*quietly, to his clerk*): I've about had enough of this. Is he sober?

TEWKESBURY: Perfectly, sir. And my hearing is perfect too.

MAGISTRATE (*to himself*): Oh—God!

TEWKESBURY: Now, officer, I want you to follow this next question very closely.

CONSTABLE: I follow all . . .

MAGISTRATE: Be quiet, officer. That was not a question.

CONSTABLE: Sorry, sir.

MAGISTRATE: If you will confine yourself to answering questions, and Mr Tewkesbury will confine himself to asking material ones, we may get on.

TEWKESBURY: That would be an ideal cross-examination, if I may say so, sir. But (*shaking his head sadly*) *Non cuivis homini* something something *Olympum*.

MAGISTRATE: *Corinthum*, Mr Tewkesbury. *Contingit adire Corinthum*.

TEWKESBURY: Bless my soul, sir. I beg your pardon. I must be slipping. *Quantum mutatus ab illo Tewkesbury.*

MAGISTRATE: This isn't a Latin class. Please get on.

TEWKESBURY: If you please, sir. To resume, officer, when did you last see a person annoyed?

For a fraction of a second the constable looked at the magistrate and then hastily withdrew his eyes.

CONSTABLE: I'm not sure.

TEWKESBURY: Well, be sure, officer.

MAGISTRATE: How can he be?

TEWKESBURY: He can tell me the last occasion he *remembers* seeing anyone annoyed.

MAGISTRATE: That's a different question.

TEWKESBURY: Then I ask it. And remember, officer, you're on oath.

CONSTABLE (*after a slight cough*): I saw a pedestrian this morning annoyed by a motorist.

TEWKESBURY: How did he show his annoyance?

CONSTABLE: He shook his fist.

TEWKESBURY: Excellent, constable. He shook his fist.

MAGISTRATE: Don't repeat the answers, please, Mr Tewkesbury.

TEWKESBURY: I was savouring it, sir.

MAGISTRATE: Well don't.

TEWKESBURY: And when was the last occasion before that when you saw someone annoyed?

CONSTABLE: I cut myself shaving this morning.

TEWKESBURY: And what did you say, officer? You may say it in Latin if you prefer.

MAGISTRATE: You may not.

CONSTABLE: I said 'damn,' your Worship.

TEWKESBURY: Excellent. Damn. I'm so sorry, sir. I was savouring again. And the time before that?

CONSTABLE: I can't be sure I get the order right.

TEWKESBURY: Of course not, officer. You couldn't possibly be expected to remember such things in correct order. *Lex non cogit ad impossibilia.* Well, constable, let us have another example of someone being annoyed.

CONSTABLE: I once saw someone slip and fall down in the street. He said 'bloody hell,' as far as I remember.

TEWKESBURY: And the next? Your wife perhaps has burned herself in the kitchen, or dropped something?

CONSTABLE: I broke a plate the other day.

TEWKESBURY: And what did she say? You may write it down if you like.

CONSTABLE: She called me a clumsy lout.

TEWKESBURY: Admirable. And the next, please. Did your mother or father never hit you if you annoyed them?

CONSTABLE: I was smacked occasionally.

TEWKESBURY: You were a good child, no doubt, officer?

CONSTABLE: Normal, sir.

TEWKESBURY: And at school perhaps you have seen a master get annoyed?

CONSTABLE: Sometimes, sir.

TEWKESBURY: Can you think of any particular incident?

CONSTABLE: I saw one throw a book at a boy once. It missed.

TEWKESBURY: Thank you, officer. Well, that will do for the moment. You have given me six examples of people being annoyed. And now, officer, will you be good enough to tell me what the man did in this case? Did he shake his fist? Did he say 'damn' or 'bloody hell' or 'you clumsy lout'? Did he smack my client or throw a book at her? Did he do any of these things?

CONSTABLE: No, sir.

TEWKESBURY: But you say he appeared annoyed?

CONSTABLE: Yes, sir.

TEWKESBURY: Then I'm afraid I must trouble you for some more examples, officer.

MAGISTRATE: How long is this going on for?

TEWKESBURY: Well, sir, that depends on what the officer says. I am proposing to take him through every example of a person being annoyed that he remembers. And I then propose to ask whether the man in this case did any of those things.

MAGISTRATE: Why d'you say the man appeared annoyed, constable?

CONSTABLE: He just did, sir. The look on his face.

TEWKESBURY: But you had never seen the man before, officer, had you?

CONSTABLE: No, sir.

TEWKESBURY: Then he may have had a twitch? Or an itch? Or he may have just thought of something disagreeable. How can you be sure that he was annoyed? He said nothing, he did nothing, and you'd never seen his face before. You can't be sure he was annoyed with my client, can you?

CONSTABLE: I thought he was.

TEWKESBURY: But you're not absolutely sure?

CONSTABLE: Not absolutely.

TEWKESBURY: Then you're not sure?

CONSTABLE: I'm sure but not absolutely.

TEWKESBURY: I'm afraid that's impossible, officer. If you're sure, you're sure, aren't you?

CONSTABLE: I suppose so.

TEWKESBURY: You're sure, aren't you?

CONSTABLE: I suppose so.

TEWKESBURY: Well, if you're sure, you're absolutely sure, aren't you?

CONSTABLE: Not necessarily.

TEWKESBURY: Well, if you're not absolutely sure, you mean you're not quite sure?

CONSTABLE: I suppose so.

TEWKESBURY: Then the truth is that you think the man was annoyed but you're not quite sure. (*To the Magistrate*) I can go on for some time, sir, but I respectfully submit that I have now disposed of this little matter. If the constable isn't quite sure, your Worship certainly can't be.

MAGISTRATE: I think there's a doubt. Case dismissed.

TEWKESBURY: I'm much obliged to your Worship. (*In a whisper*) Don't be too annoyed, constable.

Angela tore herself away from Mr Tewkesbury with difficulty. The next call she paid was at London Sessions, where once more, she had to admit to herself, she stayed less on her father's mission than for relaxation. There she found Mr Sumpter Hedges in the full flow of his eloquence. She soon discovered that, although Mr Hedges had no difficulty in finding his voice, the barrister in John Mortimer's little classic, *The Dock Brief*, was much too near a reality for the liking of those who want criminals to be adequately defended. Mr Hedges was addressing the jury in a case where his client was accused—most properly— of receiving goods knowing them to have been stolen.

'Members of the jury,' Angela heard him saying, as she came in, 'you are men and women of the world. Suppose this had happened to you. Put yourself in my client's position. Not his present position in the dock. I would not suggest to you, members of the jury, that any of you would ever find yourselves there. But his position at 10, Elephant Road, when he came into the house and found these cartons of cigarettes in his room. Sixty thousand of them. What would you have done, members of the jury? My learned friend for the prosecution sneers at my client's explanation of what he did. But that is what the prosecution is for.

CHAIRMAN: It is nothing of the sort.

HEDGES: Please don't interrupt.

CHAIRMAN: I shall always interrupt when you make improper remarks.

HEDGES: Then I shall leave the court.

CHAIRMAN: Continue with your address, Mr Hedges, and behave yourself.

HEDGES: I shall try again, members of the jury, but only for my unfortunate client's benefit. I was saying, when the Chairman thought fit to intervene, that my learned friend sneered at my client's explanation of what he did. Well, what would you have done? Why must the worst motives always be attributed to everyone? That is what the world suffers from today. Too little charity, too much suspicion. Why must every unusual action, every unusual event be presumed to be in bad faith? My client, who was once in the tobacco trade, finds these cigarettes in his room. Now, if you had once been in the tobacco trade, what would you have thought? It would have been different if they had been oranges and apples, or silk stockings. But they were not. They were cigarettes. And, members of the jury, I shall not be straining your knowledge of the world if I ask you to reflect that cigarettes form the bulk of the tobacconist's trade. Indeed that is admitted. Mr Jones, whom I cross-examined on the subject, agreed that, so far from cigarettes being a strange thing to a tobacconist, they are in effect his life-blood. Well, members of the jury, my client comes home and finds his life-blood on the floor. What more natural than that he should put it in the cupboard? My learned friend suggests that my client ought to have gone to the police. Why on earth, members of the jury? Why should he assume that there was something sinister about these cigarettes? What does a tobacconist expect to find on his premises? Iron bars, members of the jury? Flowers? Chimney pots? No, members of the jury, tobacco, and, above all, cigarettes. And now, if you please, members of the jury, the prosecution suggests that, because a tobacconist finds that a normal delivery of cigarettes has been made, he ought to assume that they have been stolen. At this rate no retailer could accept any deliveries without going to the police.

CHAIRMAN: I'm sorry to interrupt you again, Mr Hedges, but I cannot allow you in your enthusiasm to try to mislead the jury. The accused is not a tobacconist and never has been one. Twenty years ago he spent three months as a boy in a tobacconist's shop. He is not a shop-keeper at all. He is a window cleaner. He found the cigarettes, so he says, in the sitting-room of the house where he lodges. It is a private residence, not a shop.

HEDGES: Very well, my Lord, I shall retire from the case.

And, throwing his brief down on to the desk with a bang, Mr Hedges stalked out of court.

Angela waited to hear how the situation was resolved. The Chairman asked the prisoner what he would like to do—to carry on with the case himself, or to have an adjournment and a retrial with another barrister to defend him.

'I think I'll plead guilty and be done with it,' said the prisoner. 'I wanted to from the start.'

From London Sessions Angela went to the High Court, where she was relieved to find that the standard of advocacy was higher. First she sampled Mr Justice Storer's Court. The judge was speaking as she went in.

'I suppose you're relying on these cases, Mr Brownlow,' she heard him say, and then go on to mention the names of six cases dating from the eighteenth century down to 1950 and to give all their references correctly. Angela could not, of course, be sure whether the cases were relevant or the references correct but, as counsel stood saying nothing, she asumed that they were. The judge then went on to refer to eight other cases and to quote from three of them. Counsel remained silent. The judge continued. Angela even began to wonder if she were seeing things and if the judge were really counsel and counsel were the judge. Certainly Mr Brownlow appeared to have one of the qualities which Angela had under-stood from friends was useful in a judge, the ability to keep quite quiet. Mr Justice Storer, on the other hand, appeared to be a remarkably good advocate. For, having put Mr Brownlow's case fully, as far as the law was concerned, he then proceeded to deal with the facts, and, there again, all Mr Brownlow ever said was, 'Yes, my Lord,' or 'If your Lordship pleases.' He once tried to say: 'Your Lordship is putting it so much better than I could have done,' but Angela could not tell that he was going to say that, as all the words after 'Your Lordship' were drowned in the further remarks of the judge.

Angela began to be extremely sorry for the other side, who, she gathered, was a lady called Mrs Perkins, represented by a young barrister called Space. But she soon found that her fears were quite groundless. For, as soon as Mr Brownlow had completed his almost entirely silent submission, and Mr Space had got up to reply, the judge proceeded to tell Mr Space what his argument was and to quote, Angela again assumed correctly, just as many cases as he had quoted in favour of Mr Brownlow. On Mr Brownlow's behalf the judge had certainly convinced Angela and had appeared to convince himself that the whole of English law and all the best English judges were ranged entirely against Mrs Perkins. But, once Mr Space was standing up, all the cases quoted by the learned judge appeared to show that the law was firmly established, by all the judges who mattered, in her favour. And, when it came to the facts, the same thing happened.

'And you would say, Mr Space, I suppose,' said the judge, 'that, unless your client is telling the truth, the evidence of the plaintiff himself doesn't make sense?'

'Indeed, yes, my Lord,' Mr Space managed to slip in.

'A very good way of putting it. Thank you, Mr Space,' said the judge.

Eventually, when Mr Space considered that the judge had nothing more to say, he sat down.

Thereupon, Mr Justice Storer gave judgment.

'I am most indebted,' he began, 'to counsel on both sides for their succinct and admirable arguments. But, if

I may say so, each of them appears to have omitted several important considerations both of law and fact.'

The judge then began to refer to a dozen other cases which he had not so far mentioned, and to point out that it was really in those cases that the law applicable to this particular dispute reposed. He then proceeded to arouse that part of the law out of its sleep and, in a few well-phrased sentences (which, though of inordinate length, never got out of hand), he showed that neither Mrs Perkins nor her opponent really knew what was legally good for them.

'It is unfortunate,' he added, 'that the plaintiff did not plead this case in trespass. Had he done so, very different considerations might have applied. He could then have relied upon an entirely different line of authority.'

Having quoted eight cases in support of this proposition the judge, rather sadly, it seemed to Angela, sent them about their business with an almost curt:

'But, as I have said, that aspect of the matter does not arise.'

But, if the plaintiff had blotted his copybook by not pleading his case in trespass, the unfortunate Mrs Perkins had done no better. For she had failed to put forward the defence of 'leave and licence.' Had she done so, that would have temporarily resuscitated another eight cases. The judge referred to these, not, as he said, because they were really relevant to the matter he had to determine but so that, if the case should happen to go to the Court of Appeal, that Court would appreciate that he had those cases well in mind.

By the time Mr Justice Storer had finished, Angela had come to the erroneous conclusion that she had heard the names of all the cases that had ever taken place in the English Courts. She was wholly unaware that Mr Justice Storer had only quoted a tiny percentage of the cases which his mind obstinately refused to forget.

Angela also formed a great admiration for the unbiased way in which the judge appeared to be determined, at one and the same time, that the plaintiff should win the case and that the defendant should not lose it. But, although she thought that this was a signal example of British fairness and of the complete impartiality of the English Bench, she felt somehow that Mr Justice Storer was not quite the man for her father. Judges, she remembered, were supposed to hear and determine cases. Admirably as Mr Justice Storer no doubt determined his cases, she did wonder when he actually heard them.

In the next court she tried, she arrived during counsel's closing address. He sounded an able man and seemed to have an extremely good case. He ended his speech with:

'And so, my Lord, with some confidence I ask you to find for the defendants.'

Whereupon the judge, without troubling counsel for the plaintiff to argue, gave judgment against the defendants for the full amount claimed by the plaintiff.

'Mr Barnstaple has, with his usual eloquence, endeavoured to persuade me to take a different view of the transaction. In my opinion there is nothing in his argument at all. Indeed, it is plain beyond a peradventure that the plaintiff's claim is made out. The only matter which has occasioned me any surprise is that the action was defended at all. The defence was doomed to failure from the start.'

Angela decided that Mr Barnstaple was not the barrister her father wanted. She realised that she was not able to judge of the merits of the case, but the point she took against Mr Barnstaple was his use of the words 'with some confidence.' If he did not know that he was going to lose the action, then, in view of the terms of the judgment, it showed that he must have a lower standard of intelligence than she at first thought. Alternatively, if he realised that he was fighting a hopeless battle, it was silly of him to use the cliché 'with some confidence,' when he had in fact none.

Next she went into one of the Courts of Appeal which, at that particular time, was more like the Centre Court at Wimbledon, except that there was no applause. A singles match between two Lords Justices was in progress. Each was using Counsel rather like a ball boy, while the presiding Lord Justice acted as umpire.

'I suppose you say to that,' said Lord Justice Keen to Counsel for the appellant, 'that that point was never taken in the Court below and is not open to the respondent now?'

'I do, my Lord,' said counsel, dutifully supplying Lord Justice Spenlow with the ball.

'What about paragraph 6?' asked Lord Justice Spenlow, making the chalk rise on the sideline.

'That quite plainly is only dealing with equitable estoppel,' replied Lord Justice Keen.

Before counsel could pick up the ball, Lord Justice Spenlow picked it up himself and returned it at speed with:

'Isn't that what we're talking about?'

'No,' said Lord Justice Keen.

By now the ball boys were standing almost idle, though ready to pick one up, whenever required.

'This is 1958 not 1872,' said Lord Justice Spenlow.

'Might I respectfully suggest,' said the presiding Lord Justice, 'that if we continue much more on this topic it will be 1972 before we reach the main point of the case.'

Lord Justice Keen immediately queried the umpire's decision, which can be done with more decorum in Appeal Court One than at Wimbledon.

'The rules of pleading must be observed,' he said.

'And the rules of common sense, fairness and justice,' replied Lord Justice Spenlow.

Counsels' heads were now moving much like the spectators' at the side of the Court at Wimbledon.

'And those rules require that a party should put his case fairly into writing, so that the other side knows what he has to meet.'

'Personally,' said the presiding Lord Justice, 'it seems to me that that has been sufficiently done in this case.'

Angela translated this immediately into 'Fault called.'

She never learned what the case was about. She realised that it involved intricate matters of law, which laymen cannot be expected to understand. Nor could she judge of the ability or resilience of mind of the judges, as she could not follow the subject-matter with which they were dealing.

She went out into the corridor. She was standing there, looking a little disconsolate, when a young barrister in robes approached her.

'You look lost,' he said. 'Can I help you at all?'

'How kind,' said Angela. 'I wonder if you could.'

'What Court are you looking for?'

'As a matter of fact, I'm looking for a judge, not a court.'

'What's his name?'

'I've no idea.'

'That does make it difficult. Can you describe him?'

'Not physically. But he's the best you keep. Quiet on the Bench, quick, but not too quick, at understanding what's said to him.'

'By "not too quick" I suppose you mean that he doesn't interrupt counsel before he's finished a sentence, by saying: "I suppose you mean so-and-so," when, if he'd let him finish, he'd have found out that counsel meant nothing of the sort?'

'That's right,' said Angela. 'And he doesn't object to new ideas and doesn't ask questions if he knows the answers. In fact, as I said, he's the best judge you've got, full of learning but not parading it, courteous, kind, firm, with a mind of his own but ready to listen to other people's views before he comes to a conclusion. In which Court shall I find him?'

'Well,' said the young man, 'I'm not a judge yet, but meantime I think Halliday's the man you want. He's in Q.B.3 today. I've just done a case in front of him.'

'Would you mind telling me your name?' asked Angela. 'I might want a barrister one of these days.'

'I'm sorry to hear that.'

'I've nothing special in mind, but one never knows. And you've been very kind.'

'I'm afraid that doesn't necessarily mean that I'm any good at the Bar.'

'Aren't you?'

'It's difficult to tell. I don't think I'm bad, but then I shouldn't be much use if I did. I can't be good yet, as I haven't been going long enough.'

'Well, if you can tell a good judge when you see one, that must be a recommendation.'

'Oh, everyone knows Halliday. What he says today the House of Lords says tomorrow. He's for stardom. The only question is where and when.'

'That sounds like my judge,' said Angela. 'Could you tell me which way to go?'

'I'll take you there, if I may.'

'It is good of you.'

'Not at all. I should like to.'

On the way to Court 3, Angela asked her guide when she could have the chance of hearing him in action.

'I don't often come here,' he said. 'I'm mostly in the County Court at present. Don't suppose you'd be interested, but I'm at Hampstead tomorrow.'

'Could I come?'

'Well, of course, but I can't conceive why you should want to. Now here we are.'

Angela found that the qualities of Mr Justice Halliday

had not been exaggerated to her. There was no doubt at all about it. This was the judge her father wanted. He might have been made to measure. She had succeeded in one part of her task. Now for the other. She wondered about her companion.

'You haven't yet told me your name,' she said.

'It's Southdown as a matter of fact, Charles Southdown. May I be introduced?'

'I'm Angela Walsh. How d'you do? You've been a tremendous help to me. I am grateful. May I come to Hampstead tomorrow?'

'I'll call for you and drive you there if you like.'

'No, I won't let you do that,' said Angela, 'though it's extremely kind.'

She was not particularly anxious to disclose that she was the daughter of Lonsdale Walsh, and, as she still lived in his house, disclosure would in all probability be necessary if the young man called for her. It was not that she was ashamed of her father. He had told her that his conviction was based on perjury and she believed him implicitly. But it was sometimes embarrassing and she hated people being sorry for her.

They walked along the corridor. Charles pointed to a Court.

'Old Boniface is in there,' he said. 'He tried Lonsdale Walsh, you know. Oh, of course, your name's Walsh. No relation, I suppose?' he added with a laugh.

CHAPTER FIVE

Caught up in the Machine

WHEN Lonsdale heard from Angela that she had found his judge and that she had considerable hopes that she had found a barrister too, he went into conference with Spikey and began to formulate his plans in greater detail.

Spikey listened with the happiest anticipation. When Lonsdale had finished Spikey said:

'Now, the bloke you want is the Boss.'

'Can he be trusted?'

'Now, look, guv. Do you trust me?'

'Would I be telling you all this if I didn't?'

'Right, you wouldn't. Then why do you trust me, guv?'

'Because I think you want the money and, provided there's enough money and not too much risk, there's no reason not to.'

'Right. Well, the Boss is the same. If he likes the job and the pay's right, 'e's safe as me aunt's grandmother and she died ten years back.'

'Good. Where is he now?'

'Well, unless 'e's 'ad a bit of bad luck, 'e's out at the moment; going straight they call it.'

'All right, Spikey. You go and see him as soon as you get out and tell him what we want. My daughter will give you all the money you need. I've already told her that you'll be calling on her when you get out and that

she's to give you all the help you ask for. She'll understand that but, just to be on the safe side, try to smuggle
this out with you.'

Lonsdale gave him a minute piece of paper on which he
had written: 'And I mean all.'

'Angela will look after you and the Boss all right. Now,
the only thing is, how are you to let me know?'

Spikey winked.

'You'll know all right,' he said, 'if your daughter under-
stands this note. There ain't a prison wall which fifty
nicker won't go through—and less,' he said.

'Right,' said Lonsdale. 'Well, I hope it won't be long
now.'

Some little time before, Angela had gone to the County
Court to hear Charles perform. She had formed an immediate liking for the young man and realised that she must
guard against prejudice in his favour. She did not precisely
know why her father needed his services, but she was
quite determined not to recommend anyone just because
she had a liking for him. Her father had said, however,
that experience was less important than intelligence and
mental resilience. So he was certainly a possible. But she
was taking no chances and proposed to listen to him in
action, even more critically than she had listened to the
others.

She arrived at the County Court and sat in the public
benches as near the front as possible. Judge Smoothe was
presiding, an elderly man of a kindly disposition; not a
profound lawyer, but with a keen sense of justice and a
desire to do the right thing between the parties. Moreover,
he was not simply anxious that the result of every dispute
should be fair but that it should, as far as possible, also be
satisfactory to both parties. In consequence he was known
at the Bar as 'Old Settlement,' for, in a very large number
of cases, he persuaded the parties to agree to a compromise
judgment. He did not always realise that, though such

behaviour on the Bench may be of great value, it is a two-edged weapon. In a good number of the cases where, as a result of the judge's desire to satisfy everyone, the case was settled, the consequence in fact was that no one was satisfied. Judges and lawyers are good at trying to heal wounds and bring warring parties together and they are often successful, but it is important to ensure that this method of approach is not used or pursued to the end in inappropriate cases.

Sometimes Judge Smoothe would smile happily to himself, as he disrobed, about a settlement he had procured, and even make a remark on the subject to the usher who was assisting him.

'Very satisfactory, don't you think, Walters?'

'Very satisfactory indeed, your Honour.'

Naturally Mr Walters always agreed with his judge, but there was no sycophancy about it at all. He had been the judge's usher for many years and it was not strange that they began to think alike. Indeed, the usher could have given most valuable advice to the parties in many of the cases.

'Much better than fighting it out,' the judge went on. 'No one would have gained. A lot of mud slung, probably another day's costs incurred and no one any the better off.'

'Very lucky they had you to try it, your Honour. I'm not sure that the parties always appreciate what you do for them.'

This was unconscious humour on Mr Walters' part, because at that very moment both counsel in the case were having the greatest difficulty in parrying the verbal blows of their respective clients.

'I came here to get my rights,' said the plaintiff. 'And what have I got? A bloody sausage.'

'Well, you did agree to the settlement,' said his counsel timidly.

'Of course I agreed. What else could I do with the old basket looking at me over his spectacles and telling me I'd bloody well got to?'

Judge Smoothe had not put it so indecorously, but unquestionably the plaintiff had got the point correctly. What the judge had in fact said was:

'Of course, if the plaintiff wishes me to try the case, I will do so. That is what I am here for. But I think he would be wise to bear in mind that no case is won until judgment is given, and, even then, it may be reversed on appeal. Moreover, even if the plaintiff should win, would it give him real satisfaction to live in the same house as a person over whom he has triumphed? Injunctions between neighbours do not make for good relationship. A friendly smile is worth far more than damages. I repeat that, if the plaintiff is prepared to take the risk of losing, or of winning and finding it a barren victory, I will, of course, proceed with the hearing. But don't you think it would be wise, Mr Gathermore, if the plaintiff consulted you before taking the final decision?'

'Bloody well settle,' is certainly shorter but it is not the way judges talk.

On the day when Angela went to Judge Smoothe's court, Charles was appearing for the defendant in a case where a lady had somehow or other got her hair tangled in a washing machine. She complained that the machine was unsafe or alternatively that there ought to be a warning on it that people with long hair should tie it up before using the machine. Fortunately her hair was not torn off and her main complaint was the shock which she had suffered. Her husband had come into the kitchen just in time and cut off the current. The plaintiff now said that she was too nervous to use the washing machine, and that in consequence she had either to do the washing in a tub, which took much longer, or send it out, which was more expensive. In addition she and her husband said that instead of being a happy, gay young woman, she had become moody and irritable.

'I hope,' said Charles, when he rose to cross-examine her, 'that I shan't irritate you too much. I shall try not to do so. Tell me, Mrs Small, do you feel irritated at the moment?'

'I feel nervous.'

'A lot of people feel like that in the witness box,' said the judge, 'and I'm not surprised. I'm only surprised at how calm most of them appear on the surface. Would you like to sit down while you give your evidence?'

'No thank you, your Honour.'

'What form does your irritability take?' went on Charles.

'I just feel irritable.'

'And how do you act when you feel irritable? Do you bite your husband's head off?'

'I wouldn't say that.'

'Well, that's something. Do you jump if you hear a bang?'

'Yes, I do.'

'And didn't you before the accident?'

'I don't know. I suppose I did.'

'Do you burst into tears suddenly for no reason?'

'I wouldn't say that.'

'Then what form does your irritability take? I've made a few suggestions. Can you help me at all about this?'

'I just feel irritable.'

'Could anyone tell that you feel irritable?'

'I don't know. I suppose so.'

'Why do you suppose so? Unless you do something to show that you're irritable, how should anyone know that you are?'

'I don't really know—now you put it like that.'

'Perhaps "irritable" is the wrong word. Perhaps you just have bouts of being moody and depressed? Is that right?'

'Yes, perhaps it is.'

'I suppose that happened to you occasionally before the accident, as it happens to most people?'

'I suppose so.'

'If you get a large award of damages in this case, do you think you will feel less depressed?'

Before the witness could answer, Judge Smoothe intervened.

'I don't think that's quite a fair way of putting it, Mr Southdown,' he said. 'The witness hasn't said she's depressed at the moment, only that she's nervous.'

'I'm sorry, your Honour,' said Charles. 'Do you feel depressed at the moment, Mrs Small?'

'It's all so strange here, I don't really know.'

'Did you feel depressed yesterday then?'

'Not all yesterday.'

'Then did you feel depressed at some time yesterday?'

'I think I did.'

'When?'

'I can't be sure.'

'Why did you feel depressed?'

'I don't know really.'

'Were you thinking about the case?'

'I may have been.'

'That depressed you?'

After a further short cross-examination about her shock and extra expense, Charles turned his attention to the question of liability. Within a very few minutes he had tied up Mrs Small in much the same way as the washing machine had tied up her hair. And half an hour later Judge Smoothe, in giving judgment for the suppliers and manufacturers of the washing machine, said this:

'There seems to be an impression today that, if someone is injured, someone else has got to pay. I cannot conceive any other reason for this action being brought. It was doomed to failure from the start. The accident was obviously due entirely to the plaintiff's carelessness. There was nothing whatsoever wrong with the machine. As for the suggestion that there ought to be a warning notice on the machine, you might as well suggest that the manufacturers of the machine should supply a nursemaid with every machine. If you bang your head against a wall it will hurt. If you hang your hair over moving machinery, of course it may get caught up in it. The case is too plain for argument. I can only hope that the depression which may descend on Mrs Small as a result of this judgment may be of short duration. My advice to her is to forget all about it and to start using the washing machine again. But she should keep her hair up when she does so, charming as it must look when it is loose.'

At the close of her day in Court, Angela was satisfied that, in spite of his inexperience, Charles would do as well as anyone for her father. She wrote and told him so. Within a short time of his receiving the letter, Spikey was released and things began to happen.

CHAPTER SIX

Invitor and Invitee

SPIKEY called on Angela the day after his release, and produced the note from her father.

'How much d'you want?' she asked Spikey.

Spikey told her.

'What d'you want all that for?'

Spikey told her.

'I see,' she said, 'and when is all this going to happen?'

'That depends on the Boss, Miss. 'Aven't seen 'im yet. 'E may 'ave some other engagements. But I don't suppose 'e'll be long. 'E's got to get everyone organised, though. You can't rush these things.'

But, though things were not rushed, they happened, and, as a direct consequence, Douglas Broadwater received a telephone call which, though it pleased his wife, was a very great surprise to them both. Douglas had been Treasury Counsel at the Old Bailey for some years and he had in fact been one of those engaged for the prosecution against Lonsdale. Mary Broadwater was very anxious for Douglas to become a judge in due course, and she complained to him from time to time that he did not attend legal gatherings enough. She believed—quite wrongly—that, by associating regularly with the right people, Douglas would increase his chance of promotion to the Bench.

Douglas was not a particularly sociable person, and did not care for garden parties, cocktail parties, or the like. Indeed, he did not much care for going out to dinner.

He was an able man at his job and had few other interests, except reading. He and Mary were very happily married and their disagreement on the subject of going out and about did not disturb their happy relationship. But Mary never stopped urging Douglas to do what she wanted.

They were both equally surprised at the telephone call, but Mary was delighted.

'You'll accept, of course,' she said, and on this occasion Douglas did not feel that he could refuse, though he was completely astounded at the invitation. He had answered the telephone and been told that Mr Justice Halliday wished to speak to him. He had appeared before Halliday on a number of occasions but he did not know him personally and he could not conceive why the judge should suddenly telephone on a Thursday evening. That was odd enough, but the conversation was even more odd. For Halliday had invited Douglas and Mary to come and spend the week-end with him. If he had not clearly recognised the judge's distinctive voice, he would have imagined that a practical joker was responsible. But there was no doubt about it. It was Halliday speaking. It was true that the judge apologised for the shortness of the notice and added that he had been wanting to invite them for some time but had never got round to it, but it was none the less one of the most extraordinary things that had ever happened.

'I just can't understand it,' he said to Mary. 'He doesn't know me. We don't belong to the same club. I don't think we've ever met out of Court. Why on earth should he invite us? It doesn't make sense.'

'Well, I don't know why it is,' said Mary, 'but it's a jolly good thing. He's just being sociable, I expect. Probably thinks that the Bar and the Bench should get together a bit more. You remember this when you're a judge. I'm glad I was in the room when he phoned, or I believe you'd have refused.'

'I must say he made it very difficult for me to say "no." It was almost like a Royal Command. What time shall we start?'

Mr Justice Halliday was a bachelor who lived in a house in the country called Howard House. It was not far from London. He had made a very large income at the Bar in the days when a man could retain a reasonable proportion of his earnings after paying income tax and surtax, and his attractive house stood in the middle of about ten acres of land. As Douglas and Mary drove up the long drive they were still discussing the possible reason for their visit.

'I wonder what a policeman's doing outside the front door?' said Mary, as they were driving up to it.

'I expect he's had a threatening letter or something,' Douglas suggested.

The judge opened the door to them himself and welcomed them.

'I'm afraid you must have thought it a bit odd being invited at the last moment, but I'm delighted you could come.'

He was about to show them to their room, when Douglas suddenly remembered an important telephone call that he needed to make.

'I'm so sorry, judge,' he said, 'but might I use the telephone?'

'Whom d'you want to phone?'

'A chap in London.'

'I'm afraid not,' said the judge.

Halliday had no reputation for meanness, but Douglas could only assume that he grudged the amount of the toll call.

'I'm terribly sorry to be a nuisance,' he said in a somewhat embarrassed voice, 'but the call is rather important and—and—of course, I'd want you to let me pay for it.'

'That's beside the point,' said the judge. 'I'm afraid you can't use the telephone, and that's all there is to it.'

'Well,' said Douglas, 'I'd better go down to the village and make it. It is rather important. I want my clerk to alter a conference for Tuesday.'

'Tuesday will keep,' said the judge.

'But I'd really like to let him know now, judge, and if you'll forgive me . . .'

'I'll forgive you certainly,' said the judge, 'but you can't go down to the village, and there we are. Shall I take you to your room?'

CHAPTER SEVEN

The House Party

MILES HAMPTON, who was one of the witnesses for the prosecution at Lonsdale's trial, had had a varied life. He had never been very successful. Possibly his greatest success was in the witness box at the Old Bailey, where he withstood all the efforts of defending counsel to make him deviate from his original story. He came out of the box in the same good state and condition in which he went in. No sweat pouring down the face; no glass of water for him; he required no assistance from the judge. As calmly as his jerky method of speaking allowed, he told his story, and one juryman actually said quietly to his neighbour:

'Well, he's obviously telling the truth.'

And so it appeared. Yes, it had been a good day for Miles Hampton.

He did not have so many good days. He was the kind of man for whom no one is sorry, because he never appeared to need sympathy. One day he would be found in the Thames, or under an omnibus, and his friends and acquaintances would wonder why on earth he did it. Such a happy type. Not a care in the world. Up to a point they would be right. Apart from a desire to know where the next meal and the rent were coming from, Miles had few cares. But he took almost a childish delight in keeping up appearances. He certainly had no success at making money or love or any of the things which most people think important, but it was his ability to keep up appear-

57

ances which made people think he had nothing to worry about. He wore well-cut expensive clothes, for which he sometimes paid. Usually by instalments ordered by the local county court judge.

'But really Mr . . . Mr Hampton,' Judge Knight had said to him, 'if you can afford to go to an expensive tailor, you can afford to pay him.'

'I'm afraid that doesn't follow, your Honour,' Miles had replied blandly. 'I find it much cheaper to buy one really good suit than several shoddy ones.'

'I've no doubt you do, if you don't pay for it.'

'But I shall, your Honour, given time. Unfortunately I have been out of employment for the last three years.'

'What is your occupation?'

'I've told your Honour, none—at the moment.'

'But, when you do get a job, what sort of job do you do?'

'Anything honest within my capabilities, your Honour. I have no particular qualifications. I would take up brick-laying but I gather it's a skilled occupation. I would do ordinary labourer's work, but unfortunately I have a weak heart. I would sell newspapers but I can't get a pitch.'

'What are your qualifications?'

Miles looked down at his feet inside the witness box and then up again to the judge, as though making a swift appraisal of himself.

'I have had some administrative experience, your Honour. I was a major during the war. For a short time I was a permanent president of Courts Martial. I learned a little law then, but not really enough to become a qualified lawyer.'

'What are you living on?'

'I sometimes wonder myself, your Honour. I have had National Assistance, though I prefer to do without it when I can.'

'This is hopeless,' said Judge Knight to the creditor's

solicitor. 'Your client had better forget it. Unless you'd like to make Mr Hampton bankrupt. The debt is £60, I see.'

'I don't think that would do much good,' the solicitor had said.

'If only I could get a job I'd pay the debt at once,' Miles had said, and he meant it.

At about the time Mr Justice Halliday was showing the Broadwaters to their room, Miles was sitting in his room, wondering how to spend the day, when his landlady sent a man up to him.

'Come in,' said Miles.

The stranger came in.

'You Miles Hampton?' he said.

'That's right.'

'Ever done any crowd work?'

'Films, you mean?'

'Yep.'

'Twice,' said Miles.

'Want a job?'

Miles repressed a choking feeling in his throat. He was a sentimental person and sentimentalised about himself. This incredible answer to his needs made him want to cry. After a moment he said:

'Yes, I could do with it. How many days?'

'Three or four. Can't be sure.'

'When does it start?'

'Now.'

'How did you hear of me?'

'You're on the list.'

'Good Lord, I didn't know they were so efficient. Right. Where is it?'

'Just out of London.'

'How do I get there?'

'I'll take you.'

'That's very kind.'

'Better bring a few things. It's on location. May have to stay there.'

'O.K.,' said Miles.

Ten minutes later he was being driven towards Mr Justice Halliday's house. When they arrived, he pointed to the man outside the door.

'Real policeman?' he asked.

'You bet,' said the man, and they went in.

The same afternoon Angela telephoned Charles' chambers, and spoke to him. He was delighted to hear from her again.

'I'm afraid you'll think this very odd after our very short acquaintanceship,' she said, 'but I wondered if by any chance you'd be free this week-end. I've been asked to take someone to a week-end party. I shall quite understand if you'd rather not, but could you come?'

'I should love it,' said Charles. 'I shan't even look to see if I've any other engagements, because, if I have, I shall cancel them.'

'How nice you are,' said Angela. 'I deserved a snub.'

'Nothing of the kind,' said Charles. 'How do we go? Shall I drive you?'

'That would be lovely.'

They made the necessary arrangements and that evening Angela and Charles drove to the house of Mr Justice Halliday.

'Why the policeman?' he asked on arrival.

'Your guess is as good as mine,' said Angela, a remark which would have made her father blush.

The party at Mr Justice Halliday's house was now beginning to take shape, but there were more guests to come.

One of the witnesses against Lonsdale was dead, and his widow was at home when a cheerful stranger called on her.

'Mrs Elsie Meadowes?' he asked.

'That's me.'

'Widow of the late Kenneth Meadowes?'

'Well, I was, but I'm courting again.'

'Glad to hear it, Mrs Meadowes. I've come just at the right time.'

'Why? Who are you?'

'You go in for the pools, don't you, Mrs Meadowes?'

'I do sometimes, but never 'ave no luck.'

'That's all changed, Mrs Meadowes. You've had some luck.'

'Me? I 'aven't won, 'ave I?'

'Not in the way you expected, but you've won just the same.'

' 'Ow much?'

'Well, I'm not sure, but I'll explain. Although we get a lot of winners on our pools, we want to encourage the people who don't win. So we've decided that a certain amount of the money will be set aside and a prize given out of it each week to certain losers selected at random. And you're one of the lucky losers, Mrs Meadowes. Congratulations.'

He held out his hand.

'Well I never. About 'ow much will it be?'

'Well, not less than a hundred pounds—perhaps more.'

'Well, if that ain't the best thing I've 'eard since Jimmy got the compensation. When do I get it?'

'Now—if you come with me. The first award is going to be made in person.'

Half an hour later they were on their way to Mr Justice Halliday.

' 'Ere, where is this?' said Mrs Meadowes. 'And what's a copper doing 'ere?'

'To see that no one pinches the stuff. Come along in, Mrs Meadowes.'

The late Mr Meadowes had had a good deal to do with

judges, who had imposed varying sentences upon him, but he would never have imagined that his widow was actually going to be entertained in a judge's house.

The house party was now nearly complete. One of the prospective guests, Herbert Adams, was difficult to find, but he was traced in the end. He was on a bench in the park. Two men approached him.

'Herbert Adams?' said one of them.

'Well?' said Adams suspiciously.

'We're police officers,' said one of the men, 'and we want you to come along with us to answer some questions.'

'I ain't done nothing,' said Mr Adams.

'Then that's all the better for you,' said the man. 'Come along.'

And Mr Adams, without further protest, walked with the men to a car and was soon being driven to Mr Justice Halliday's house.

'Wot's this?' he said on arrival. 'This ain't a police station.'

'It's temporary,' said one of the men. 'While the other's being repaired.'

Jo Barnwell lived in an attractive house in the Regent's Park area. She was just leaving it when a small boy dashed in front of a car, narrowly missed it and then fell flat on the pavement and remained still. She at once ran to him. The boy was motionless. A fat man was getting out of the car. He helped Jo to lift up the boy. He seemed unconscious and his face appeared to be covered with blood.

'We'd better take him to the hospital,' said the man. 'I wonder if you'd mind helping?'

'Of course not,' said Jo.

Together they lifted the little boy into the car.

'I wonder if you'd mind sitting with him while I drive?'

'Certainly.'

The man got into the driving seat and drove off. He stopped at the corner and two other men got in. One got in beside the driver and the other in the back.

'Which is the nearest hospital d'you think?' the fat man asked Jo.

Jo told him, but her attention was mainly taken up with the boy. So she did not notice for a few minutes that the car was not going towards the hospital she had mentioned.

'You're going the wrong way,' she then said.

'I know the house surgeon at the hospital we're going to,' said the driver.

As Jo had not seen the small boy rehearsing his part that morning several times, and covering his face with red paint, she did not become suspicious until the car was nearly out of London.

'Where are you going to?' she asked eventually. 'This boy ought to be seen to at once.'

'He's O.K.,' said the man next to her. 'All right, Tommy, you can wake up now.'

Tommy sat up and grinned.

'Now don't make a fuss, madam,' said the fat man. 'You'll be quite all right, if you behave. But it's three and a half to one, and chloroform's a nasty business. We might give you too much.'

'Where are we going?' she asked.

'You'll see.'

And in due course Jo found herself at Mr Justice Halliday's house. She was momentarily relieved to see the man at the door.

'Officer,' she called.

'Yes, madam,' he said, coming up to them.

'I've been kidnapped by these men,' she said.

'Well, if you'll go through the front door and take the first door on the right, they'll take all particulars.'

Jo had not fully taken in this extraordinary behaviour

by the policeman when her companions took her into the house.

One hour later another car drove up to the house, and Lonsdale got out and walked swiftly inside. A companion followed more slowly, after saying to the man at the door:

'That's the lot, I think.'

CHAPTER EIGHT

Address of Welcome

HALF AN HOUR later the guests were all assembled in the drawing-room, when Lonsdale came in.

'I might have known it,' said Jo.

'Evening, Jo, nice to see you,' said Lonsdale. 'Now, if you're all comfortable, I'll explain. First of all, let me apologise to you all—particularly to you, Sir George, for the somewhat unusual methods I have been compelled to adopt.'

'I hope you realise,' said Mr Justice Halliday, 'that, although you are undergoing a sentence of imprisonment for life, you can not only be sentenced for your present crimes with a sentence to begin after your life imprisonment is over . . .'

'That is hardly a deterrent, Sir George,' interrupted Lonsdale.

'You know quite well what I mean. A sentence of life imprisonment is reviewed after ten years and normally the convicted person is released after serving anything from ten years to fifteen years. What I was going to add was that conduct such as yours will presumably result in your serving the maximum sentence for your original crime, in addition to the further sentence which I mentioned.'

'That is a risk I must face,' said Lonsdale, 'but let me say at once that, as far as most of you are concerned, I do very much regret the steps which I have had to take. But I venture to suggest that you must agree that there was no alternative open to me. Now, what are the facts? Eighteen months ago I was convicted of the murder of Adolphus Barnwell. I was convicted on perjured evidence. There is the woman who procured my conviction by that evidence.'

'There stands the man who murdered my husband,' said Jo.

'Don't interrupt please, Jo,' said Lonsdale. 'You'll have plenty of time to say your piece later. After my conviction, I appealed to the Court of Criminal Appeal. My appeal was dismissed. I petitioned the Home Secretary, to no avail. I asked my Member of Parliament and other friends to have my case reviewed. It was hopeless. Nothing could be done. Now, Sir George, would you mind assuming, just for one moment, just for the purpose of argument, that in fact my conviction was procured as I have said. What other course was open to me? For most people there would have been no alternative but to suffer the sentence. But I was able to do something else. Admittedly I have had to break the law in order to do so. I have had to escape from prison and to induce all of you by one method or another to assemble in this house. You, Sir George, I have very regretfully had to make a prisoner in your own house. None of you I hope will suffer any more discomfort than is absolutely necessary. You will, I am sure, understand that every precaution will have to be taken to prevent you from communicating with the outside world. No one is going to come here looking for an escaped convict. But all the necessary steps have been taken to deal with friends and tradesmen who may call or telephone. None of you will suffer in the slightest degree, provided you make no actual or apparent attempt to get help. The judge has pointed out that my offences are already such that I have really nothing to fear from any further crimes which may be committed by me or on my behalf. So I do beg you all to be sensible and to make no show of resistance.

'Now, why are you here? Most of you will have guessed. We have the transcript of my trial, photostat copies of the documents, all the chief witnesses, except one, who gave evidence, and the lady who paid them. Now don't interrupt, Jo. You know you did. I am proposing, with the assistance of the two members of the Bar present, to go through the whole of the evidence at my trial in such a way as to satisfy the judge that what I have said is true. If, after this new trial, as I may call it, the judge is satisfied that my conviction was properly procured, I shall give myself up to the police and take the consequences of my actions. But if, as I am quite confident I can do, I satisfy him that hardly a word of truth was spoken at my trial, then I hope that in those circumstances the judge will take such steps as he thinks proper to put the matter right. I shall certainly surrender to the police, but I venture to suggest that no one can then fairly complain at my unorthodox methods of showing that the jury in returning their verdict of guilty were grossly misled. How long this trial will take I naturally cannot say, but in the intervals between the sessions every endeavour will be made to make you as comfortable as possible. Now, are there any questions?'

'What do you want us to do?' asked Broadwater.

'I should like you to be kind enough to conduct the case on behalf of the prosecution, and your learned colleague, Mr Southdown, to conduct the case on my behalf. I apologise for the absence of any solicitors to instruct you but, in the circumstances, I'm sure you won't mind interviewing the witnesses yourselves. It may be of some help to you if I say that, while the witnesses whom Mr Broadwater will see will tell him all manner of lies, I shall tell Mr Southdown nothing but the truth.'

'Mr Walsh,' said the judge, 'if this affair is going to serve any useful purpose, I should advise you to stop persisting in saying that your case is right and the prosecution's is wrong. It doesn't impress me in the least. Dozens of rightly convicted criminals say the same thing, when they are trying to get off on appeal. It has no value at all.'

'Thank you for your guidance, Sir George,' said Lonsdale. 'I will try to benefit from it. But I hope you will understand that the reason I emphasise these matters is because I feel very strongly about them. I have been in prison for eighteen months as a result of lies, and she knows it.'

'There you go again,' said Mr Justice Halliday.

'I'm sorry,' said Lonsdale. 'Now, I suggest that we have dinner shortly and go to bed early. In the morning Counsel on each side can get his instructions and by, say, twelve o'clock, they should be ready to present the case to you, Sir George. Will that be convenient to you all? Good. I take silence for consent. Spikey, could you arrange about drinks?'

CHAPTER NINE

No Escape

L ATER that evening the judge explained to Charles and Broadwater how the whole thing had started, as far as he was concerned. On the Thursday evening he had been dining by himself when his manservant informed him that a police inspector would like to see him. He was shown in at once.

'I'm so sorry to disturb you, my Lord,' he said, 'but the police have just received some urgent information. It may be a hoax but we don't think it is. I don't know if you remember sentencing a man called Thorowgood—an inappropriate name, if I may say so, my Lord—for robbery with violence? He got seven years.'

'You must tell me more about the case if you want me to remember. Names mean very little to me,' said the judge.

'Well, either at the trial or down below in the cells, he was heard to swear vengeance against you. He said it was an unfair trial and an unfair sentence and, to use his own words, he was going to get you.'

'I can't say that I remember anything about it,' said the judge, 'but convicted people do sometimes shout threats. As far as I know, no attempt has ever been made to carry them out.'

'That's right, my Lord,' said the man, 'until tonight.'

'What has happened?'

'Thorowgood has escaped.'

'I've seen nothing about it in the papers, and there's nothing on the wireless.'

'I know, my Lord. In view of the information we had, it was decided not to assist the man in any way. You see, my Lord, when it's published that a man has escaped, something has to be put in the papers as to the steps being taken to recapture him. You know the sort of thing, my Lord—his house is being watched, or a search is being made in the woods near so-and-so, or it is believed that he escaped in a small blue car heading for the North; road blocks are being established round a wide area. That information may be true or false but, whichever it is, it gives the man something to think about. Now, if nothing is said at all, it makes him jittery to begin with. The silence must worry him. Where are they searching? What are they doing? Indeed, has his escape been discovered yet? And so on.'

'Yes,' said the judge, 'but where do I come into all this?'

'My Lord,' said the man, 'there is another very special reason why we don't want to publish anything at the moment. We have pretty reliable information that not only is he heading in this direction with a view to carrying out his threat, but that he is going to be accompanied by several armed men to assist him. They're a very determined gang, and the police are very anxious to catch the lot. With your Lordship's assistance, I think we can. Would your Lordship tell me who lives in this house?'

'I live here with a cook and a manservant only,' said the judge.

'Trusted servants?'

'I've had them for years.'

'I don't want to alarm your Lordship, but we have information that two masked men were in Brocket Wood, five miles from here. What the police would like to do, if your Lordship will permit it, is to fill this house with plain clothes police officers, themselves masked, and wait until the attempt is made. We then hope to get the lot.'

'What's the object of the masks?'

'Well, my Lord, we believe that there are about ten or more men in this, coming from different directions. If one of them sees a masked man he will at once assume that he's one of the gang.'

'But mightn't it be dangerous for your own men, if one of them mistook one of his colleagues for one of the gang?'

'That's all been provided for, my Lord. They will wear a special type of mask and, of course, in addition there's a password.'

'I see,' said the judge. 'Well, it's all very odd, but, if that's what you want to do, I suppose I'd better let you do it. But I hope you won't make too much mess.'

'You leave that to us,' said the man. 'Thank you very much, my Lord. I'd be grateful if you and your staff would all go into one room above the ground floor, so that we can give you complete protection.'

'All right,' said the judge. 'When d'you want to start?'

Ten minutes later nine masked men were admitted into the judge's house, while he and his cook and manservant chatted in one of the bedrooms.

Not very long afterwards, the "inspector" came into the bedroom.

'There's been a bit of a mistake,' he said. 'Thorowgood hasn't escaped after all.'

'Good,' said the judge. 'Then we can go downstairs again,' and he led the way to the drawing-room. In it were eight masked men.

'You might remove those things now,' said the judge.

'I'm afraid this is going to be a bit of a shock to you,' said the man who had fetched the judge, 'but we are not policemen.'

'Then who are you?'

'That doesn't matter,' said the man, 'but I'd better tell you what is going to happen. We are going to hold you and your staff prisoners and the house will be in a state of siege. But, provided you do what we tell you, no harm will come to any of you. On the other hand, if there is the slightest attempt to escape or call for help, I cannot be answerable for the consequences. Is that understood?'

'I hear what you say,' said the judge.

'Good,' said the man. 'Now, first thing in the morning, you will telephone to the Law Courts and say that you're not feeling very well and won't be able to sit that day and possibly not for a few days longer. If, in the course of that conversation you attempt to give the alarm in any way, it will be the worse for all of you. And you might bear in mind that none of us can be identified. You may have been surprised to notice that the uniformed man you first saw had a beard. Unusual in a police officer. And glasses. No doubt you'll be able to tell the police the colour of his hair and his approximate height. Any other information you give will be quite valueless.'

'What is the object of this outrage?' asked the judge.

'You'll learn in due course. The next thing you must do is to telephone to a Mr Broadwater, a barrister, and ask him and his wife to stay here for the week-end.'

'And if I refuse?'

'Don't,' said the man.

There was a slight pause, and the man turned to the cook and said in a somewhat menacing tone:

'You don't want him to refuse, do you?'

The cook thereupon fainted.

'You see,' said the man. 'She'd like you to telephone, and so should we. Shall I get you the number?'

'But I don't know him, or his wife.'

'You must make some excuse for asking him. After all, you're a judge and he's a barrister. He'll want to come. I expect he's appeared in your court from time to time.'

And so it came about that the judge telephoned and invited Broadwater and his wife for the week-end.

CHAPTER TEN

Conversation Pieces

AFTER the judge had explained what had happened, he lowered his voice and added:

'There is one thing we can do. I've done it already, as a matter of fact.'

'What's that, Judge?' asked Charles.

'Well, it's only a possibility, but it's worth trying. But it depends on the wind. I've written several notes calling for help, and, if there was a bit of a breeze, thrown them out of the window. One of them went quite a long way.'

'Did you see what happened to it?'

'I did,' said the judge. 'It was eaten by a cow.'

'We can all try it,' said Charles.

'Don't do it unless a wind gets up. Otherwise they'll just drop down and may be found.'

At that moment Lonsdale came into the room.

'I hope you're not finding things too inconvenient,' he said. 'If there are any urgent messages you want to send to anyone, I'm sure it can be arranged—provided you make no attempt to give an alarm.'

'How long do you propose to keep us here?' asked the judge.

'No longer than is necessary,' said Lonsdale. 'How long d'you think it'll take? The first trial took two days. This shouldn't take much longer. Perhaps not as long.'

'I can't think what good you imagine it will do you,' said the judge.

'Well,' said Lonsdale, 'without wishing to appear

73

impertinent, you should. Supposing I did satisfy you that the whole case against me was a fake. What would you do?'

'I don't feel called upon to answer that question,' said the judge.

'Well, of course not,' said Lonsdale. 'There's no reason why you should answer. But I can't conceive that any judge, who was satisfied that there had been a verdict procured entirely by perjury, would do nothing about it, just because he only learned of the fact through completely unlawful means. You'd do something about it, wouldn't you,' he said, turning to Broadwater, 'if you were a judge? And you?' he added, to Charles.

Both of them took their lead from the judge and said nothing.

'Well, it doesn't matter,' said Lonsdale. 'I've enough faith in you all to make me think this is worth doing. You all loathe injustice, and I'm quite sure that, if any of you saw what you believed to be a gross piece of injustice, you would take all the steps you could to have the matter put right. Almost anyone in the country would. And, whatever people may say about lawyers, I'm quite sure that they'd be the first to try to remedy an injustice they'd heard of, if they knew there was no one else who could do anything about it. Well, I mustn't detain you any longer, gentlemen. You know where you are sleeping, I think. I hope you'll have as good a night as possible.'

Lonsdale next paid a call on Jo. She was in bed reading.

'Forgive me for not knocking,' he said.

'I forgive you for nothing,' said Jo. 'Why did God make you such a bloody man?'

'My dear Jo, that's a line of enquiry which it would suit few people to indulge in. Even you, for instance. He'll have quite a lot of questions to ask you, when you get up there.'

'Thanks for saying "up".'

'I don't believe there's a down. We all go to Heaven.

The only difference is that some of us won't like it. You, for instance, you won't find anyone to fight.'

'What about you? You fight hard enough.'

'That's only to get my way, not because I like it. You enjoy a fight for its own sake.'

'Perhaps I do. I'll put you back in gaol if it's the last thing I do.'

'You won't have to, Jo. I shall go back on my own, as soon as this is over.'

'I'll get you back before it's over if I can, and I'll see you stay longer when you do get back.'

'They may not ask you, Jo. Granted you put me there, it's not your business any longer. It'll be up to the judge then. It's up to me at the moment. What does it feel like to be in my power? Do you love every moment of it? It must be a new experience.'

'A very unpleasant one.'

'But you don't really dislike me—not really—any more than I hate you.'

'That's all you know.'

'But I do, Jo. I do know. If I were standing on the edge of a precipice you'd push me off as soon as look at me. But all the same, if things had been different, you'd have pushed the other fellow off instead. We'd have made quite a pair, you know. And I've never pretended I didn't like you.'

'Funny way of showing it.'

'It's a funny world. But it's true. I like you very much, Jo. And you like me.'

'I've a funny way of showing it.'

'True enough. May I kiss you?'

'I'm in your power, aren't I? What's to prevent you?'

'I shouldn't dream of kissing you by force. I told you, I hate fighting. I only fight when there's something I want to get.'

'That's hardly a compliment.'

'I don't pay you compliments, Jo. Not that kind anyway. I *am* paying you the compliment of having an extra guard outside your window.'

'Why the window?'

'Just in case you thought of sending any little notes into the air. We like to keep the grounds tidy.'

'You don't seem to have made much headway with the judge.'

'How could you expect me to, yet? But you wait.'

'I am waiting,' said Jo.

And they kissed.

At about the same time Angela was paying a visit to Charles. She was very apologetic.

'You do see my point of view, don't you?' she said. 'I know my father is innocent. He never lies. Wouldn't you have done the same?'

'I can't conceive the situation arising. But, when you say you know he's innocent, how d'you know? Most wives who are fond of their husbands believe them innocent. So would most children their parents. The courts have found him guilty and the Home Office can find nothing even to merit an enquiry. Why should they all be wrong?'

'He would never have, pleaded "Not guilty" if he'd been guilty.'

'There you are wrong. It isn't telling a lie to plead "Not guilty". It is simply calling on the prosecution to prove your guilt.'

'Well, anyway he's told me he's innocent and he's never told a lie in his life. I do want you to believe that.'

'How d'you know he's never told a lie?'

'Because I do. Because I've lived with him all my life and you can't live with someone without knowing these things. He just can't tell a lie. You're going to appear for him and I do want you to understand that.'

'Why? What difference can it make?'

'All the difference. If you don't believe in his case you may not bother.'

'Of course I will,' began Charles, and then stopped and laughed.

'What's the joke?'

'I said "of course I will" automatically, as though this were going to be a real trial.'

'It's going to be a very real trial,' said Angela.

'You don't understand. In an ordinary case in the Courts it doesn't matter to me if I believe my client innocent or guilty. I put up the story he tells me for better or worse, whether I believe it or not. And pretty well everyone does the same. If a criminal's counsel had to believe in his innocence before he could raise any enthusiasm for the defence, there'd be precious few enthusiastic defences put forward, and most of those would be put forward by pretty stupid advocates. If your father's were a real case, I'd do the best for him I possibly could, whether I believed him or not. But this case is different. So that really you're quite right about it this time. If I really believed your father to be innocent, I should try much harder tomorrow. In any event, of course, I'll try sufficiently hard to prevent one of your bodyguard knocking me on the head. But I suppose that's all I'm prepared to do. Now if I really thought he was in the right, I would have a go.'

'Well, thank Heaven I came to see you,' said Angela. 'You must believe me. Why d'you think he'd take all this trouble, spend all this money and risk getting many years of extra imprisonment, if he weren't innocent?'

'I'm afraid that argument can always be raised. It's sometimes said that there are two kinds of judges. One kind think that a plaintiff wouldn't spend the money on bringing an action unless he thought he had a good claim, and the other kind think that the defendant wouldn't defend unless he had a good defence. And the commonest cry by an obviously guilty thief in the witness box is:

"What should I want to steal it for?" No, I'm afraid that sort of argument doesn't cut any ice with me. I'm much more impressed with your obvious complete trust in your father. I say "obvious" but I should say "apparent." I don't know you well enough. How do I know that you're not putting on an act?'

'You're very frank.'

'No point in being anything else.'

'Well, I can only give you my word. Mark you, I'm not a truthful person like father. I don't mean that I'm an inveterate liar. I'm just normal. Like you, I expect. But father's not. He's quite abnormal. He just never tells a lie, never, never. Please try to believe me.'

'You certainly sound as though you meant it, but, if I accept that, how can I tell that you're right?'

'Well, do I strike you as a fairly intelligent person?'

'Very.'

'Thank you. Well, then, if I am above average intelligence, surely I'm either putting on an act as you suggest, or I'm probably right? Obviously I can't ask you to be certain about it. I can only beg of you to think that what I'm saying may be true. You were quite right. This is not a real trial. But it's vital to us, and, if you believe in our case, it must be some help.'

'Well,' said Charles, 'I'll promise you this. I will go into it with an open mind and then, if I find in the course of the case that you appear to be right, I'll do my damndest. I can't say more than that.'

'No,' said Angela, 'I don't think you can. Thank you for being so sweet. Have you told the judge, by the way, that it's really your fault that this is happening to him? I chose you myself, but, if you hadn't told me to go and see the judge at work, I might never have heard him.'

'Well, I haven't yet,' said Charles. 'I think I'll wait till it's over.'

'Tell me,' said Angela, 'if we are right, and if we

satisfy the judge that father is innocent, he will do something about it, won't he? He won't just let father go back to gaol and say "serve him right for making such a nuisance of himself"?'

'No, I don't think he'd do that. If you ask my honest opinion, I don't believe for a moment that you'll do any good at all, but if I'm wrong, and if you really showed that your father's innocent, then I'm quite sure that the judge would do something about it. We all would, if it came to that.'

'Father was sure of it.'

'It's the first hurdle you've got to get over. And I don't believe you ever will.'

'But you will try?'

'I will, but you mustn't expect anything.'

'But I do.'

'Why are you so certain?'

'Because I think the truth's bound to come out the second time. You'd say that it usually comes out, wouldn't you?'

'I don't know about usually, but often, certainly.'

'Well, I can't believe that it won't this time.'

'Well, good luck, anyway. At any rate I should never have met you but for this.'

'Are you pleased?'

Charles paused.

'Yes,' he said eventually. 'In spite of being kidnapped and locked up and threatened with I don't know what, I'm pleased.'

In what might be called the guards' common-room, Spikey was holding forth on the beauties of a life of ease.

'No more cops,' he said. 'No more stir. I wouldn't 'ave believed it if 'e 'adn't told me 'isself. Didn't know there was so much money in the world.'

'How d'you know that he'll keep his word?'

' 'Ow do I know! 'E's done all right so far, 'asn't 'e? If
we didn't get no more we shouldn't do so bad. But I know
'im. 'E'll do wot 'e's said.'

The advantage of Lonsdale's infirmity of always telling
the truth was that he normally carried conviction with
people, even in the most unlikely places.

'Thou shalt find no ease neither shall the sole of thy foot
have rest,' put in one of the guards, known to his friends
as Holy Hal. He had spent many years in prison and the
Bible had had a great attraction for him there. Not from
a religious point of view. He simply enjoyed the language.
He did not quote it either hypocritically or in order to
moralise. Possibly he enjoyed showing off his immense
knowledge, but his real pleasure was to relate everyday
words and actions to phrases in the Bible for his own
benefit. No doubt saying it aloud and creating an impression among his friends and acquaintances gave him added
pleasure, but that was not the real source of his enjoy-
ment. It cannot be said that he ever deliberately went
back to prison to devote more time to his study, but this
was hardly necessary. Like most habitual criminals, he
was not very successful and usually found his way back
there soon after his release. Some prison chaplains found
his knowledge a severe test of their own. One of them, in
the hope that it might lead to better things, actually
played a sort of Bible chess with him. Everything they
said had to come directly out of the Bible from the beginning to the end. Any failure to reply with a quotation lost
two marks. Any mistake lost one more. The parson had
to confess that he looked forward to his visits.

'Why not look on the bright side?' said another of the
guards, to Holy Hal.

'We wait for brightness, but walk in darkness,' said
Holy Hal.

'O.K.,' said Spikey, 'but it's round the corner. Me and
the missus'll go travelling, I think.'

'Do they put your previous on a passport, like they do on a marriage certificate?' asked another guard.

They discussed the pleasures of life and the various ways in which they would seek them out. Lonsdale had indeed put a very large sum aside for the purpose of paying the men without whose help he could not succeed. He was prepared to spend half his fortune or even more on ensuring the success of his scheme. Angela had already opened an account for the Boss, in which she had placed £100,000 to be distributed among them all equally, with an extra bonus of £10,000 for the Boss himself. Her father had promised another £110,000 to be paid on the completion without interruption of his new trial. Lonsdale did not consider that £220,000 out of a million was a penny too much to pay for the chance of freedom.

Naturally suggestions of this kind were taken most seriously by the Boss and his associates. Spikey had been quite right that the Boss was the man Lonsdale wanted. The combination of a public school and University with a prison education produced an interesting result in the Boss. He could mix happily in all circles. Among criminals he was trusted because he never deliberately let them down. His part in a crime was the organisation. He seldom appeared himself—except in the dock. One of the things his associates liked about him was that, if they were caught, he didn't try to wriggle out and leave them to take the rap. Naturally, if the police never came to him, he was not expected to go to them. But he did not do what so many receivers do when questioned by the police (and later in the witness box), throw the entire blame on his accomplices.

This tendency on the part of receivers is a great help to the prosecution in some cases. When there is a charge against a number of people of conspiring to steal, everyone knows that usually one of the accused is the receiver and the remainder are the thieves. The prosecution put the receiver first on the record, so that he has to go into the witness box first. He attempts to give a display of wide-eyed innocence and, without the slightest hesitation, he throws on the thieves any blame there happens to be going round. In their indignation the thieves trip into the witness box and sink themselves and the receiver. The result is that, even if there isn't much evidence against the receiver at the beginning of the case, there is at the end— all provided by the defence.

The Boss naturally tried to avoid conviction, if possible, but never at the expense of his friends. His public school had done something for him.

He was a kind of independent contractor in crime. Some hostesses, when giving a party, instead of employing direct labour and buying the food themselves, employ a caterer to do the lot. The Boss was the equivalent of the caterer. If you wanted, for example, to crack a safe, or carry out an important warehouse robbery, he would supply everything, the men, the materials and the method. Naturally, he only took on jobs of sufficient size. He didn't supply buns and cups of tea for the Mothers' Union Summer Party. He would do the equivalent of a small dinner party for six, if it was exclusive enough, but in round figures he would not touch anything if there was not at least £1,000 for himself, not subject to tax.

He was against unnecessary violence, but he recognised that neither banks nor ordinary citizens would part with their valuables without sufficient inducement. Accordingly, when an exploit could not be carried out entirely in secret, which he preferred, he authorised the use of enough violence to achieve the object. But he always emphasized the necessity for as much care being exercised as possible. For example, gagging can be a very dangerous operation, and he had two specialists (who had been male nurses) who knew how to complete this delicate and sometimes difficult operation with as little discomfort as possible and no danger to the patient.

When in funds, the Boss went to expensive restaurants, where his cheques were gladly accepted. He never dishonoured a cheque, though his bank manager did sometimes wonder where the cash came from. Particularly did he wonder about this on one occasion, a month or so after his own branch had been robbed of over £10,000. Did Mr Bostock's payments-in come, as he said, from winnings at the races? How lucky for the Boss that he was not like Lonsdale. Otherwise, presumably he would have had to tell the manager that it would have avoided a lot of trouble if he had just transferred the amount to his account before the robbery. It would have saved an elaborate and quite expensive plan, and the temporary disablement of a bank messenger and two policemen. It is sometimes difficult for a bank manager to decide whether to open an account for a man whom he knows to have convictions against him, or to keep the account open after a conviction. Just because a man has been convicted, he should not be denied ordinary services when he comes out of prison. Obviously, if the account is considered unsatisfactory, or there is something suspicious about the cheques paid in, the account will be closed. But the Boss's account was always conducted most satisfactorily. He never overdrew. On the contrary he normally had a large credit. Any cheques paid in were from obviously satisfactory sources, and, though most of the payments-in were cash, that is the case with many course bookmakers. And he always ascribed these payments to winnings at the races. The Boss would never have been so indiscreet as to pay in the proceeds of a robbery the day after it had taken place. It would have given him some amusement to return to his bank, for the credit of his account, the money he had stolen from it, the day after the robbery, but he had been to gaol sufficiently often to curb his sense of humour on that occasion. When he did pay in a large sum a month after the robbery, the cashier did say to him:

'Had a good day, Mr Bostock?'

'One of the best,' the Boss had replied.

'I can't think why people bet,' said the cashier.

'People are very stupid,' said the Boss, 'fortunately for me.'

'Well, I suppose we all are if it comes to that,' said the cashier. 'If we'd been more careful we should never have lost that £10,000 a month ago.'

'I don't know what else you could have done,' said the Boss. 'Tell me, what other precautions could you take?'

'We're taking them, Mr Bostock,' said the cashier. 'But walls have ears, even in a bank, you know.'

'Well,' said the Boss, 'I expect they're unnecessary anyway. No one would go for the same place again so soon.'

'That's a comfort,' said the cashier. 'The messenger will be pleased to know that.'

'I hope he's all right,' said the Boss. 'I was very sorry to read about it . . . but there it is, it's a wicked world and these things will happen.'

'Well, it's nice to know they won't happen here again for a bit. I wonder what I'd do if a gunman suddenly walked in?'

'Now—what *would* you do?' asked the Boss. 'You ought to have a foot button you can press so that the doors close automatically and an alarm bell rings.'

'That's an idea,' said the cashier. 'Thanks very much. I'll pass it on. I wonder why we've never thought of that before?'

'Of course,' said the Boss, 'the chap might get cross and try to shoot his way out. I should just have the alarm bell if I were you and leave the doors open. But, you know,' he added, 'there's only one thing that will keep a really determined burglar out.'

'If it's not a breach of confidence,' asked the cashier, 'what might that be?'

'Don't have anything worth stealing inside.'

'Oh—that's an old one,' said the cashier.

'I know,' said the Boss, 'but it's the only one that works. Good morning.'

The Boss had made the arrangements for Lonsdale's escape and retrial, with great care and efficiency. He had even gone to the lengths of arranging diversionary escapes at two other prisons, in the hope of providing employment for as many police cars as possible at the time of Lonsdale's escape. It had been a simple affair. Everything in these matters depends on exact timing. Three minutes were allowed for the whole operation. At the appointed moment a small car drew up to a particular place outside the prison wall. The street on which the wall abutted was not used a great deal and the precise spot which had been chosen could only be seen for about fifty yards in either direction. Between seventy-five and a hundred yards in each direction away from the place where the escape was to take place, two large lorries waited with their engines running, ready to block the road for a sufficient time at the crucial moment. At the appointed time two men got out of the small car and threw a rope ladder over the wall. Lonsdale was there, with a confederate to hold it while he made the descent. He went up quickly and down on the other side within a minute. The precise timing of the whole operation had been rehearsed most carefully several times to make sure that, as far as could reasonably be ascertained, they would have the necessary three minutes. The operation had been rehearsed without the rope ladder, so as to see that both sides were in the right place. Lonsdale was not an expert in climbing rope ladders but he made the journey safely, jumped in the car and was driven off. The two lorries never had to be used and drove away slowly behind the small car. By the time the alarm was given, Lonsdale was well out of the district, making direct for the judge's house.

The announcement of his escape was in the normal

form. 'Lonsdale Walsh, who is serving a sentence of life imprisonment for murder, today escaped from Northwall prison. A special watch is being kept at all ports and airfields.'

But not at judges' houses.

CHAPTER ELEVEN

Out of Town Tonight

ONE of the few witnesses who was quite pleased to have been kidnapped was Miles Hampton. It was true that he was not to be paid as a film extra, but he was fed and housed and it was a new experience. His life had become increasingly dim and with little or no excitement in it. Now here was certainly an adventure which he would be able to retell over pints of beer. It hardly needed any exaggeration either. Indeed, it was so extraordinary that he doubted if people would believe it. That troubled him for a moment—until he suddenly realised with a thrill that, once it was over, it would make headlines in the newspapers. That thought quickly led to another. Perhaps he would be asked to write an article. He had heard that quite a lot of money could be made that way. Then again, he might be interviewed on the wireless—or even on T.V. They might even revive *In Town Tonight*. He visualised something of this kind:

The Interviewer: Tonight we have someone who will interest viewers tremendously, someone who actually took part in the incredible proceedings in Mr Justice Halliday's house, someone who was taken for a ride, literally, and forced to give his evidence over again before the judge, literally, at the pistol point. Has there ever been such an astonishing story as was unfolded after Lonsdale Walsh eventually surrendered to the police? It was, literally, breathtaking. But you have read all about the story for yourselves and you don't want to hear any more from me.

87

You want to see the man who was made to take a part, and an important one too, in the astonishing events which fell, literally, like a thunderbolt on the legal world. So, without more ado, here is Mr Hampton. How d'you do, Miles, if I may call you that. Nice of you to come here tonight.

Miles: Not at all. I'm very pleased.

Interviewer: I expect it will be a long time before you forget your extraordinary experiences?

Miles: Yes, I expect it will be.

Interviewer: Nothing like that has ever occurred to you before, I take it?

Miles: No, that's right.

Interviewer: Not the sort of thing that happens every day?

Miles: No.

Interviewer: Tell me, what did you find the most interesting part?

Miles: The most interesting part?

Interviewer: Yes, the part that interested you most.

Miles: In what way?

Interviewer: In any way.

Miles: I don't really know.

Interviewer: But it must have been very interesting?

Miles: Oh, yes, it was, very.

Interviewer: And frightening too. I'm sure I should have been very frightened.

Miles: I wasn't exactly frightened.

Interviewer: A little nervous perhaps?

Miles: Yes, I suppose so, at first.

Interviewer: It must have been all very interesting.

Miles: Oh, yes, it was, very interesting.

Interviewer: Didn't you wonder whether you would ever be rescued?

At this stage in the interview Miles suddenly realised with a shock that, if something went wrong, if a revolver suddenly went off, or someone hit him on the head with a blunt instrument, he might never be in *In Town Tonight*, or even in the world at all. The thought stopped his imagination for a few moments, and he spoke to his companion, Herbert Adams.

'D'you think we'll ever get out of this alive?'

' 'Ow should I know?'

'I thought you might have some sort of idea.'

'Well, I ain't, see. I been in worse spots and I been in better.'

'Well, you got out of them all right.'

'That don't mean we shall get out of this one.'

'It doesn't mean we shan't.'

'It doesn't mean we shall.'

'One doesn't want to be too pessimistic.'

His companion spat out of the window.

Miles returned to his thoughts.

Meanwhile Lonsdale was preparing for the trial in the morning. He chose the dining-room as the most suitable room, and it was arranged in the most convenient manner so that, while the proceedings would not be formal as in a court, they would be conducted with reasonable dignity. Angela had brought from his house three copies of the transcript of the proceedings at his trial, one for the judge and one for each barrister. He also had photographs of the exhibits. All these documents he had obtained for the purposes of his appeal to the Court of Criminal Appeal, and were brought by Angela together with notebooks and paper for the use of the judge and counsel. He had wondered whether the witnesses should be examined on oath but, after consideration, he saw no point in it; they had already committed perjury, so it was obvious that the fact of swearing on the Bible had no effect on them. And, whatever they said, they could not be convicted of perjury, as it was not a legal trial.

Finally he checked all the security arrangements and, after being satisfied that all was well and everything ready for the trial next morning, he went to bed. He slept reasonably well. He was happy in the thought that at last he was going to be able to prove that he was convicted solely by reason of a plot. The possibility of failure never occurred to him, even though he had no clear idea of how the prosecution's case was to be broken down. He had failed in breaking it down once. Why should he succeed the second time? The witnesses were the same, except for the man who had died. They would presumably tell the same story. Unless they were shown quite plainly to be lying, the judge would obviously believe them, and all his trouble would have been to no avail. But he did not believe this could possibly happen. He had not thought it possible at his trial. He had a different defending counsel then but, though he was sure Angela had made a good choice, it was not the change of counsel that made him so certain. It was the consciousness of right. Had he appreciated how gullible the jury would be on his original trial, he might have acted differently then. But now he knew that everyone was against him, everyone except Angela. That, he felt, made his task easier. He knew what he was up against. Overwhelming prejudice. But that was at the same time his own strength. Everyone except himself and Angela would start the trial believing that it was little more than a farce. Once an inroad was made into the case for the prosecution, its fall would be all the greater, just because it had appeared originally to be impregnable. It would be a day of triumph. It must be.

CHAPTER TWELVE

Retrial

THE following morning Charles and Broadwater spent some time preparing for the case to begin. It was finally decided to have an early lunch and to start the trial immediately afterwards.

'You will, I hope, forgive a light lunch,' said Lonsdale, 'but I am anxious that none of us should feel sleepy.'

The judge did not feel called upon to comment, and Charles and Broadwater followed his lead. The cold ham and tongue and salad were eaten in comparative silence for about ten minutes. Spikey eventually broke it with:

'This ain't a funeral, is it?'

No one answered.

'Well—not if everyone behaves 'isself, it ain't,' he added.

Miles suddenly visualised himself being interviewed again. It was a most interesting lunch before the trial, he would say. Why? he would be asked. 'We had ham and tongue and salad' did not seem a very good answer. 'No one said anything' was not much better. Perhaps he could start something himself and make the lunch interesting.

'I have a feeling,' he said, 'that this has all happened to me before.'

'In that case,' said Jo, 'perhaps you'll tell us how it ends.'

'I don't actually remember if it did end. I can only seem to think of this part.'

'Well, pass the sauce, please,' said Spikey, adding: 'D'you remember that bit?'

They drank water or lemonade, and it was all over within half an hour, and then the proceedings began. Lonsdale opened them:

'I know that it isn't usual for the prisoner to start the ball rolling, except by pleading Guilty or Not Guilty, but I want to make one thing plain before we start. You know the object of this enquiry and, in order to achieve it, it is quite unnecessary that the proceedings should be conducted as at an ordinary trial. For example, there are all sorts of rules of evidence which normally have to be observed. A witness mustn't say "what the soldier said." I dare say that makes for justice as a whole. I don't know. Nor do I care. There'll be no such rules here. There'll be no objections to evidence on the ground that it isn't admissible. Everyone will have a free hand—subject only to the judge's requirements. For example, I see no objection to one witness being asked a question while another witness is in the witness box. Mr A says something; the judge or counsel can turn to Mr B immediately and ask him what he says to that. The only requirement is that the proceedings should not get out of hand and, if we all agree to do what the judge asks us to do, that aspect of the matter should be sufficiently taken care of. Does everyone understand?'

No one spoke.

'I take it from your silence that you understand what I mean,' Lonsdale went on. 'It should be a new experience for you all. Indeed, it might result in legal reforms being introduced. I won't pretend that I'm interested in that aspect of the matter. All I'm concerned about is to see that my original trial is fully investigated by every means at your disposal. Now, shall we begin? Unless the judge knows of some better method, perhaps Mr Broadwater will start by calling his witnesses for the prosecution. You have, no doubt, all read the evidence and know what the case is about. Unless, therefore, the judge wants to hear, or Mr Broadwater wants to make, a preliminary speech, I personally see no point in his opening the case. But, of course, as I have already indicated, there will be no objection to his intervening with an explanation or correction in the middle of the evidence. Indeed, all the things which you can't or shouldn't do in court can be done here, if anyone thinks they will help.'

Broadwater's first witness was a man who had been present at the murder. He gave his name as George Allwinter. He was an artist. He had been brought to the judge's house on the pretext that he was to be commissioned to paint a picture. He said in evidence that he was walking near Adolphus Barnwell's house, although he did not know at the time that it was his house. He had heard of Adolphus as a financier, but did not know anything more about him or where he lived. As later evidence showed, Adolphus was on the way from his house to the nearest pillar-box to catch the last post, at the time when Mr Allwinter was strolling along the pavement thinking about a picture—or a model, he wasn't quite certain which. He would probably not have noticed Adolphus at all in a perpendicular position, but a large blue motor car came out of a side turning, where it might have been waiting, and changed the perpendicular to the horizontal. Mr Allwinter did not actually see the impact. He had an idea of a car coming out of the side turning, of a loud acceleration, a muffled exclamation (presumably of protest) by Adolphus, and the next thing he knew was that the car had disappeared and Adolphus lay dead in the middle of the road. He was unable to take the car's number. He went across to see what he could do for Adolphus, but saw that it was hopeless. He went into the nearest house and telephoned for the police. They were soon on the scene. He gave his account to a constable, and that was really all he knew about it.

Charles then cross-examined him.

'You have known for a long time that my client is charged with murder?' was his first question.

The judge interrupted.

'Southdown,' he said, 'I see no reason why you should call this escaped convict your client. He is not your client in any sense. You are doing what you are under compulsion.'

'I'm sorry, Judge,' said Southdown. 'It slipped out. I hope you'll forgive me if it happens again. What d'you suggest I call him?'

'It is a bit difficult,' conceded the judge, 'but I must say that in the circumstances I resent the expression "client." He is a thug and a kidnapper.'

'I don't mind what I'm called,' said Lonsdale, 'provided you all do your best to arrive at the right conclusion. I shouldn't take offence if you repeated what the judge has said, and referred to me as "the thug".'

'I'll try to call him "Mr Walsh," ' said Charles.

The judge considered whether to suggest leaving out the 'Mr.' He was not one of those judges who refer to the prisoner by his surname without any prefix. But this case was different. A prisoner is presumed innocent, until he is found guilty. In the witness box he ought, therefore, to be treated like any other witness. But this man had been found guilty. He was a convict with a number.

Lonsdale sensed what the judge was thinking.

'My number's 1074, if you'd prefer that,' he said.

The judge decided to leave the matter.

'Well now, Mr Allwinter,' went on Charles, 'you know that Mr Walsh has been convicted of murder?'

'Of course.'

'And have known it for a long time?'

'Quite.'

'And before he was convicted, you knew he was charged with murder?'

'Naturally.'

'How long after you saw the incident did you learn that the charge was not manslaughter, nor killing by reckless driving—but murder?'

'I don't know exactly. When it was published, I suppose. I saw it in the papers. About two or three weeks after he was killed. I can't be sure exactly.'

'From what you saw yourself, it might just have been an accident?'

'Why didn't he stop then?'

'He could have been frightened. Have you never heard of that sort of thing happening?'

'Yes, I have, but there's all the other evidence.'

'That's exactly what I meant,' said Charles. 'You've heard or read all the other evidence. If it weren't for that, this might in your view have been just an accident, mightn't it?'

Mr Allwinter hesitated.

'Well,' he said, 'there was no one else in the road and no other vehicle. There was no need to hit him, was there? The road was wide enough.'

'He might not have seen him.'

'Driving with his eyes shut?'

'Have you never done that?'

'Driven with my eyes shut? Of course not. If I've felt sleepy, I've stopped and had a rest. But anyway this wasn't long distance driving. This was in London.'

'I didn't ask you if you'd slept at the wheel. I asked if you'd ever driven with your eyes shut?'

'When I was awake? Of course not.'

'Haven't you?' said Charles. 'I should think again. Do you always stop your car before you sneeze?'

'I can't say that I do.'

'Well, when you sneeze, you shut both eyes. And it's for much longer than just a blink. Have you never thought of that?'

'I can't say that I have.'

'Well, I should,' said Charles. 'There are circumstances when it's very dangerous for a driver to sneeze when driving. We can test it if you like. Could we have some pepper, Mr Walsh, d'you think?'

Pepper was brought and the witness was induced to sneeze.

'D'you see what I mean?' asked Charles.

Not only the witness but everyone else could see that Charles was right.

'Well, Mr Allwinter,' he went on, 'how can you know that the accident wasn't caused by a sneeze?'

'Well, it didn't look like that to me,' said Mr Allwinter.

'But you didn't see anything until after it had happened, did you? You just had the impression of a car coming out of the side turning and the next you knew was that a man was lying on the ground and the car was gone?'

'But look at all the other evidence.'

'Exactly,' said Charles, 'that's what you've been doing, looking at all the other evidence. If it hadn't been for that, you'd have had no idea how the accident happened.'

At that stage Broadwater said that he felt he must intervene.

'All this talk of sneezing is very interesting, and may indeed be profitable for those of us who drive, but it was never suggested at the trial that this death was accidentally caused by a sneeze.'

'A lot of things may not have been suggested at the trial,' said Charles.

'I think we ought to know,' said the judge, 'if you are going to suggest that death was caused by an accident. Because, if you are, we might as well save our time. I have read the other evidence. The case for the prosecution was that this was a deliberately planned murder. Either it was or it was not. Sneezes do not come into it.'

'The point is, Judge,' said Charles, 'that the only person who the prosecution suggest may have wanted to kill Mr Barnwell is my—is Mr Walsh. If he isn't guilty of murder, it may have been an accident. Suppose Mr Walsh is right, and all the other evidence you're going to hear is perjured, the fact remains that the man was killed and killed by a car.'

'I see what you mean,' said the judge, 'but it doesn't matter to you how he was killed, so long as your—this man isn't responsible.'

'All the same,' said Charles, 'it's a little help—not much, I agree, but something, to show that accident is, apart from the other evidence, a possible explanation. Of course, if this other evidence is true, accident, I agree, doesn't come into it. It was a cold, calculated murder.'

'All right,' said the judge. 'I see what you're driving at. Shall we get on? Is there anything else you'd like to ask Mr Allwinter?'

'I'd just like to ask him about this once more. The dead man was found about the middle of the road, wasn't he?'

'About.'

'It's a good wide road?'

'Yes; he could have missed him quite easily. He could have driven either side of him.'

'If he saw him.'

Fortunately for Charles, at that moment Mr Allwinter sneezed. The pepper was still doing its work.

'Quite,' said Charles. 'Or, if he wasn't paying sufficient attention as he drove, he might have seen him suddenly and hesitated which side of him to go, in case the man went that way. You know, like two people bumping into each other in the street.'

'Then he would have stopped after the accident.'

'Most people would. But some people panic. And suppose this driver had previous convictions for dangerous driving, or suppose he was disqualified at the time he was driving, those would be reasons for someone not stopping.'

D

'I suppose so.'

'Then suppose he'd just stolen the car? That would be another reason, wouldn't it? You see, Mr Allwinter, you are not able to identify the car—or the driver—are you?'

'That's true. It happened too quickly.'

'So, for all you know, it might have been a thief, a disqualified driver or a man who sneezed and panicked. You have heard of hit-and-run drivers, haven't you? Why shouldn't this have been one of them?'

'But the other evidence,' began Mr Allwinter.

'Exactly,' said Charles.

'Suppose we get on to the other evidence,' said the judge. 'You've made your point quite clearly. If the other evidence comes to nothing, Mr Walsh should have been acquitted—but, if it's to be believed—as it was believed by the jury—he was plainly guilty, as you yourself have said, of a calculated murder.'

'If you please, Judge,' said Charles, 'I only wanted to establish that, apart from this other evidence, this might have been another of those cases where a driver doesn't stop after an accident.'

'Well, I think you've established that sufficiently,' said the judge.

'I respectfully agree,' said Broadwater.

'Good,' said the judge. 'As we're all agreed, we can get on. The sooner we finish, the sooner this outrage will come to an end. At least so the . . . the . . .'

The judge could not think of the right word. Lonsdale was not 'the accused.' He had already been accused and convicted. He was not 'the prisoner,' as he was free. It was the judge and counsel who were the prisoners. He could not keep on calling him 'the escaped convict.' It was too heavy. To call him the 'murderer,' when he was at least going through the motions of investigating the crime, offended his judicial sense. He was at a loss for a word. Eventually he went on:

'At least so the man who has brought us here has promised.'

'I keep my promises,' said Lonsdale. 'But I must make it plain that I should not feel called on to keep this one, if the investigation were conducted as a pure formality. I expect the case to be gone into thoroughly to the best of your ability. I apologise for being dictatorial in this matter. But it is the whole object of the exercise. Unless I get a fair hearing here I might as well have stayed in prison.'

'Are you saying that you did not have a fair hearing in the Courts where you were tried and where your appeal was heard?' asked the judge.

'No,' said Lonsdale, 'I'm not. As far as I could see, both hearings were perfectly fair. But mistakes have been made at fair hearings before and all I say is that my case is another example of such a mistake.'

'Very well,' said the judge. 'Your next witness, please, Broadwater.'

Jo came forward and sat in the seat which was being used for the witnesses. First of all she described her husband's position, and his relationship to Lonsdale.

'They were the leaders of opposing factions,' she said, 'and matters came to a head in regard to the management of the Anglo-Saxon Development Corporation Ltd. My husband had a very good chance of ousting Mr Walsh from his control of that company. Indeed, but for his death, I have no doubt that he would have obtained the necessary support for a resolution he was about to propose for the purpose of removing Mr Walsh from his position of Chairman and Managing Director of that company. Now, a short time before that meeting, my husband brought an action for slander against this man. In the course of that action Mr Walsh had to produce certain documents, but, shortly before the day fixed for the production of those documents, the action came to an abrupt end. It came to an end automatically because my husband was killed. And here is the man who was responsible for his death.'

'Let us avoid dramatics as far as possible, Mrs Barnwell,' said the judge. 'He has been convicted and sentenced, and there is no need for you to emphasise his guilt almost every time you speak. This is not the case of a man who is assumed innocent until he is proved guilty. He has been proved guilty and it is now up to him to show that the verdict of guilty was wrong.'

'I know him,' said Jo. 'He'll wriggle out of anything, if he gets the chance. Like he wriggled out of gaol.'

'I should hardly call it wriggling,' said Lonsdale. 'I climbed up a wall, not through a drainpipe.'

'Please,' said the judge. 'This bickering will not help the investigation.'

'Did your husband receive any kind of communication from anyone about a week before he was killed?' asked Broadwater.

'He did,' said Jo. 'He did indeed.'

'What was it?'

'He received a threatening letter warning him that, unless he immediately withdrew the action he had started, the consequences for him might be serious.'

'Have you still got that letter?'

'I produced it at the trial, and I have the photostat copy which Mr Broadwater has handed to me here.'

'Before you produce it, tell me this, Mrs Barnwell. Did your husband withdraw the action?'

'He did not—neither immediately nor at all.'

'What happened next?'

'My husband received a large parcel.'

'What was in it?'

'It was a road sign which had been dug up.'

'What sort of road sign?'

'It had "YOU HAVE BEEN WARNED" on it.'

'Did your husband pay any attention to it?'

'He did not.'

'What happened next?'

'He was murdered.'

'You mean he was run over by a car,' said Broadwater, his customary fairness as a prosecutor getting the better of him.

'I mean he was murdered,' said Jo, 'by being run over, and that man paid the driver to do it.'

'That is a lie,' said Lonsdale, getting very red in the face.

'It is the truth, and you know it,' said Jo.

'It is a lie, and you invented it,' said Lonsdale.

'Once and for all,' said the judge, 'I really cannot be of the slightest use, if this is the way you're going to go on.'

'She started it,' said Lonsdale. 'She has no respect whatever for the truth.'

'You have no respect for anything except yourself,' said Jo, 'but that respect is unjustified.'

'Will you please control yourselves,' said the judge. 'If this experience does nothing else, it shows the necessity for the Courts' power to maintain order. Nothing useful can be done if these interruptions continue. Surely you can see that?'

The judge looked at Lonsdale as he said that.

'Yes, of course,' said Lonsdale, 'but I cannot stand listening to lies.'

'If your case is right,' said the judge, 'you will have to listen to a lot of them before this inquiry is over. How can I tell whether they are lies or not unless I hear them?'

'I will try to control myself,' said Lonsdale, 'but this woman deliberately tries to bait me.'

'If that is so,' said the judge, 'why do you give her the satisfaction of seeing her shafts hit the mark?'

'There are some matters on which I cannot conceal my

feelings, but I will at any rate try to keep quiet until it's my turn to speak.'

'You kept Adolphus quiet all right,' said Jo.

This time Lonsdale said nothing.

Broadwater then resumed his examination.

'Now, Mrs Barnwell,' he said, 'a few minutes ago you said that you had a photostat copy of the threatening letter, which you say your husband had received. Will you be good enough to produce it?'

Jo handed to the judge the document. It was plain that the original consisted entirely of words and letters cut out of a newspaper or several newspapers and gummed together with transparent sticky tape. The sender was obviously taking no chances. Even the envelope, which was of a cheap kind obtainable in hundreds of shops, was addressed in the same manner.

'Had you any idea who had sent that letter?' asked Broadwater.

Charles intervened.

'I don't quite know what course you want to take, Judge,' he said. 'If this were an ordinary trial I should, of course, object to such a question, which is plainly inadmissible, but in the circumstances perhaps you would prefer me not to object?'

'Well,' said the judge, 'there has been quite enough interrupting so far, I think; and in any event, when the procedure was laid down by our captor, he said that he did not want the rules of evidence to be observed. On the other hand, I really don't see how her answer is going to help me. We all know what she will say. But her saying it won't help to prove her statement or her belief true.'

'Very well,' said Broadwater. 'I won't press the question.'

'But I'd like to answer it,' said Jo. 'I knew perfectly well who had sent it. He had.'

And she looked hard at Lonsdale, with the obvious intention of provoking him to an outburst.

'Now——' said the judge warningly to Lonsdale, and Lonsdale remained silent.

'Was there anything which made you think that?' asked Broadwater.

'The substance of the letter,' said Jo. 'No one else had any reason for sending it. Although, of course, he had his lieutenants and associates—a lot of sycophantic sheep— none of them would have done such a thing, except on his orders. He was the real person who had an interest in threatening my husband. I must admit I didn't think he'd have the guts to go through with it. But he must have sent the letter, and we know from the other evidence that he did.'

'Don't let's worry about the evidence for the moment,' said Broadwater. 'Let us confine our attention to the letter itself. Can you conceive by any stretch of your imagination any other person who could have wanted to send such a threat to your husband?'

'I cannot,' said Jo. 'And if I were twice as intelligent, and thought for ten times as long, I still couldn't. He sent it all right.'

And she again challenged Lonsdale by looking at him as she said it.

This time the judge said nothing, but merely looked at Lonsdale to see if he would rise again; he did not.

'I don't think I've anything else to ask Mrs Barnwell,' said Broadwater.

'Very well,' said the judge, and invited Charles to cross-examine her.

'Mrs Barnwell,' he began, 'it is obvious that you have the most profound dislike of Mr Walsh.'

'I haven't,' said Jo. 'I know him for what he is, that's all.'

'It is certainly obvious,' went on Charles, 'that you think he murdered your husband.'

'I don't think it—I know it,' said Jo.

'Well, you didn't see him do it, did you?'

'He didn't do it himself. He got someone else to.'

'You didn't see the other man do it, did you?'

'You know I didn't.'

'Nor did you hear him tell someone else to murder your husband.'

'The fact that I didn't hear him doesn't make it any the less certain.'

'How long have you been so sure that Mr Walsh was, if not the actual murderer, responsible for it?'

'From the very beginning.'

'So, from the time your husband was killed, you were satisfied that Mr Walsh was the culprit?'

'I was. And I was right.'

'When did you first learn that your husband had been killed?'

'Within a few minutes of his death.'

'At that time you had no evidence except that he had been knocked down by a car which did not stop?'

'I had the threatening letter.'

'Yes, of course, and the road sign. But, apart from those facts, you had none of the evidence which was given at his trial.'

'Of course not. What difference does it make? The evidence is there now and was given at his trial.'

'Well, that isn't quite right, is it, Mrs Barnwell? One of the witnesses is dead, isn't he?'

'That's not my fault.'

'Of course not. But, coming back to what I was saying, at the time of your husband's death you were quite satisfied that Mr Walsh was responsible, although you had no evidence against him whatever, except the threats which you believed he sent?'

'I knew he sent them.'

'Don't let's quibble about that. You felt sure in your

own mind that he was the murderer from the very start.
Is that right?'

'It is.'

'Now, Mrs Barnwell, will you listen to this question
very carefully? You felt sure that Mr Walsh was guilty.
You're a highly intelligent woman and you knew quite
well that the mere production of the threatening letter
and road sign would prove nothing whatever against Mr
Walsh. You knew that, didn't you?'

'I never thought about it. I knew he was responsible.'

'But you also knew that he wouldn't ever be arrested,
let alone convicted, if there were no other evidence
against him.'

'I never thought about it. I assumed that the police
would do their duty and bring the murderer to justice.
And they did.'

'Did you know that all the witnesses we're going to
hear about called on the police?'

'What d'you mean? I don't understand.'

'I mean that the police didn't find those witnesses. The
witnesses came to the police.'

'What's wrong with that?'

'Nothing—if they were honest witnesses. Were they, in
your opinion, honest witnesses, Mrs Barnwell?'

The judge intervened.

'What does it matter?' he said, 'whether she thought
them honest? The jury obviously did.'

'I agree,' said Charles, 'that the jury believed them,
but I assure you that it is material to ask this lady if she
believed them.'

'All right,' said the judge. 'If you say it's material, ask
her.'

'Did you believe the witnesses, Mrs Barnwell?' said
Charles.

'When do you mean? In the witness box?'

'When else had you seen them?'

'I hadn't.'

'Then what else could I mean?'

'You ask so many stupid questions I've no idea what you mean sometimes. Of course I believed them. They were obviously telling the truth.'

'Were they?' said Charles. 'Are you sure?'

'Of course.'

'You would have done anything to bring the person you believed to have murdered your husband to justice, would you?'

'Of course I wanted him brought to justice.'

'That isn't what I asked. You'd have done anything to bring him to justice, wouldn't you?'

'The situation never arose. He was brought to justice.'

'Without your help?'

'I gave the evidence you know about.'

'Did you do anything else?'

'Nothing that I can remember.'

'You didn't by any chance see any of these other witnesses before you went to the police?'

'See any of the other witnesses?'

'That's what I asked.'

'Not to my knowledge.'

'Are you sure of that?'

'Of course I am. I may have seen you walking in the street before today, but I didn't notice you.'

'So that before these witnesses went to the police you had never spoken to any of them, so far as you know?'

'I spoke to Mr Allwinter.'

'But none of the others?'

'How could I? I didn't know of their existence, did I?'

'Didn't you?'

'I haven't got second sight.'

'But you knew, you knew—not thought but knew—that Mr Walsh had killed your husband?'

'You don't call that second sight, do you?. That was a logical and obvious deduction.'

'And then,' went on Charles, 'without any prompting from you, the witnesses came along and proved you right?'

'Without my prompting them!' she repeated indignantly. 'Are you suggesting that I . . .'

'I'm not suggesting anything,' said Charles. 'I am merely asking you questions. Did these witnesses have any prompting from you?'

'I've already told you, I didn't know them.'

'The answer to the question may be easy,' said Charles, 'but I should like it none the less. Did those witnesses have any prompting from you?'

'Of course not,' said Jo.

'You lie,' said Lonsdale.

'Really,' said the judge, 'we were getting on quite well till then.'

'I'm sorry,' said Lonsdale. 'I tried to bite my tongue, but I just couldn't. This woman is an arrogant liar.'

The judge sighed.

'She says you're a murderer, and you say she's a liar. Do you really think that's going to help me to form a view as to whether there was anything wrong with the jury's verdict? I'd better warn you that, at the moment, I have no reason whatever to believe that justice was not done at your trial.'

Jo looked triumphantly at Lonsdale.

'But, while I'm here, I will certainly go on enquiring into the matter. So do let there be an end of these silly interruptions. Now, Southdown, is there anything else you want to ask?'

'Not at the moment,' said Charles. 'But I may want this witness back.'

'She will be available,' said Lonsdale.

The next witness was Miles Hampton. He described how he had been sitting on a bench in Hyde Park, about a week or so before Adolphus was killed. A man, whom he took to be a down-and-out, was sitting on the same bench. While they were sitting there, a man of about the same height and build as Lonsdale, dressed in a morning coat and grey top hat, walked past them smoking a cigar. A little further on he stopped at a litter basket and threw something into it. The down-and-out (who was in fact Herbert Adams) got up immediately and went to the litter basket. Shortly afterwards he came back with a newspaper and the remains of a cigar. Miles could not say positively that Lonsdale was the man they had seen, but, from his general appearance, he might have been. Adams asked Miles for a light and proceeded to smoke the rest of the cigar and to read the paper which he had brought back with it. Miles noticed that the paper was curiously mutilated. It was not torn, but had many holes in it of different sizes where parts of it had been cut out. He thought nothing about it at the time, but remembered being slightly puzzled. After Adams and he had been sitting there for a further few minutes, they both suddenly noticed a grey glove which the well-dressed man had apparently dropped. Adams got up and fetched it.

'You can 'ave it for a bob,' said Adams.

'And what d'you think I could do with it?' Miles answered.

'Find the other 'arf,' said Adams, 'I'll make it a tanner.'

'No thanks,' said Miles. 'If I were you, I'd wait here for some time, in case he comes back looking for it. He might give you more for looking after it for him. Nothing more annoying than losing one glove, even if you're made of money.'

'Thanks, mate,' said Adams. 'I ain't got nothing special to do. I'll wait. Wot d'you bet 'e gives me? Is it worth 'arf a crown?'

'It's worth a good deal more than that,' said Miles. 'They're expensive gloves. But what he gives you is another matter. Some rich men are rich because they never give away anything.'

'I'll 'ave something to say if 'e don't.'

'I hope you get the chance,' said Miles.

But the well-dressed man never returned, and eventually Miles got tired of doing nothing in the park. So he got up and went to do it somewhere else. He had pretty well forgotten about the incident when he read in the newspapers about the death of Adolphus. The paragraph referred to the threatening letter and said that a man had brought to the police a newspaper and a glove which, it was hoped, might throw light on the matter. Miles, having nothing better to do, went to a police station and asked if he could help. It was soon established that the man who had brought in the paper and glove was Adams. Shown both articles by the police Miles had said that, as far as he could tell, they were the identical articles which he had seen Adams pick up.

All this evidence was elicited from Miles by Broadwater, and Charles then proceeded to cross-examine him.

'Have you ever seen this lady before?' was his first question, and he pointed to Jo.

'Oh, yes,' said Miles.

'When did you first see her?'

'When did I first see her?'

'Yes.'

'I can't be absolutely sure, but I believe it was at the police station. I think she was there, but I can't be quite sure. It may have been the police court.'

'Had you ever seen her or spoken to her before you went to the police station about this case?'

'Had I seen or spoken to her before?'

'That's what I asked,' said Charles. 'And what is the answer?'

'Before I first went to the police you mean?' asked Miles.

'That's right,' said Charles. 'Hadn't I made my question plain?'

'I just wanted to be sure,' said Miles. 'No, I'd never seen her before.'

'Or spoken to her?'

'Well, you can't speak to a person without seeing them.'

'What about the telephone?'

'Oh, of course, I'm sorry,' said Miles. 'No, I hadn't spoken to her on the phone.'

'Or communicated with her in any way?'

'I didn't know her.'

'Or communicated with her in any way?' repeated Charles.

'No,' said Miles. 'I didn't know of her existence before this case.'

'That may be,' said Charles. 'The case started with a man being killed, and what I want to know is, how soon after he was killed did you speak to Mrs Barnwell?'

'I don't know that I ever have spoken to her.'

'Do you say that you never have?'

'Well, I can't be absolutely sure. We were at the police court and possibly the police station together, and you know how it is when witnesses in a case are waiting in the same room. They may speak to each other. I may have done. I expect I did. But I can't be certain.'

'You do a little acting, don't you?' asked Charles.

'Yes, occasionally.'

'Are you doing any now?'

'Acting?'

'Yes.'

'Well, I haven't any engagements at the moment.'

'I didn't mean that,' said Charles. 'I meant are you acting at the moment—in this room?'

'Acting what?'

'Acting a part?'

'What sort of part?'

'The part of an apparently honest, entirely independent witness.'

'That's what I am,' said Miles.

'You really saw all this happen in the park?'

'Naturally, or I wouldn't say I had seen it. I may have made a mistake about a detail or two, but the substance is right.'

'What is your present financial position?'

'I can manage.'

'How much have you in the bank?'

'I don't use my account much.'

'Is that because the bank won't let you?'

'Well, they do prefer me to have a balance before I draw a cheque.'

'When did you last draw a cheque?'

'I couldn't say. Some time ago.'

'What have you been living on during the period since Mr Barnwell was killed?'

'Oh—one thing and another, you know. I have managed.'

'Did you have a bit of luck, by any chance, just before or just after Mr Walsh's conviction?'

'A bit of luck? How d'you mean? What sort of luck?'

'Any kind of luck. Did you have a lucky bet on a horse, for example?'

'What horse?'

'Any horse. Is it a fact that at or about the time of the trial your financial position improved, if only temporarily?'

'My financial position always improves,' said Miles. 'It can't do anything else. Rather a pleasant position to be in really. Things can never get worse with me. They can only get better. How few people can say that. I find it very reassuring.'

'I gather from that,' said Charles, 'that there is no time when you would not find a present of £50 or so most welcome.'

'Well,' said Miles, 'there are about forty million people in this country, aren't there? There must be darned few of them who wouldn't find £50 useful at any time.'

'I take it you are not one of the few?'

'No,' said Miles, 'I could always find a use for £50.'

'Then you would have found a use for it at the time of the trial?'

'I tell you, I would have found a use for it at any time.'

'Did you in fact get some kind of payment at or about that time, either £50 or more or less?'

'From whom?'

'From anyone.'

'I can't recall it.'

'But, if it had happened, you could certainly have recalled it?'

'Indubitably.'

'Then why didn't you simply say you hadn't had it?'

'I did.'

'You said you couldn't recall it.'

'Precisely, because it didn't happen. If it had happened, I should have recalled it. As it didn't happen, I didn't.'

The judge looked at his watch.

'I don't know how long I'm expected to sit,' he said, 'but d'you think we could have a short adjournment now?'

'Of course,' said Lonsdale. 'I ought to have thought of it. Refreshments will be available in the drawing-room.'

CHAPTER THIRTEEN

Interlude

'Ow d'yer think it's going, guv?' asked Spikey, after they had left the court room.

'It isn't going at all yet,' said Lonsdale, 'but then I never expected it would. But I like that young man who's appearing for me. I fancy he's shown two of the witnesses anyway a red light.'

'But 'ow are you going to show that they're telling a pack of lies, guv?'

'It'll come with a rush, Spikey. You'll see. They're telling lies and they know it, and they know we know it. One false step by one of them and we'll break the whole thing wide open. You wait, Spikey, you just wait.'

Meanwhile the judge was having a quiet word with Charles and Broadwater.

'There was a wind this morning,' he said, 'and with luck someone'll pick it up.'

'I sent one too,' said Broadwater.

'Good,' said the judge. 'This farce has gone on long enough.'

'Judge,' said Charles, 'I'm not absolutely sure that it is a farce.'

'You're not at the Old Bailey now, old boy,' said Broadwater. 'No need to keep up appearances.'

'I'm not,' said Charles, 'but I shouldn't have gone half so far as I did today, if I hadn't thought that there mightn't be something in it. Admittedly, if this were a real trial I should have felt pretty uncomfortable at some of the questions I put, but I should have had to put them just the same. Something my client—I beg your pardon, Judge—something Walsh has told me has made me think very hard.'

'Don't overdo it, old boy,' said Broadwater.

'Oh, well,' said the judge, 'we shall see. And it's certainly good practice for you. How long have you been called?'

'Nearly seven years, Judge.'

'Have you really? Wish I showed my years as little. But you can't be thirty yet.'

'Not quite.'

At about that moment a small boy about a mile away from the judge's house had just picked up a piece of paper. It said in block capitals—SEND POLICE AT ONCE TO MR JUSTICE HALLIDAY'S HOUSE, HOWARD HOUSE.

It was signed by the judge himself. The small boy could not read but he entertained himself by tearing the small piece of paper into very much smaller pieces. Then, like Mr Justice Halliday, he threw them to the winds. Meanwhile, the piece of paper sent by Broadwater had stuck in a hedge in a lane.

Miles approached Jo while she was having a drink.

'How am I doing?' he asked.

'Don't ask silly questions,' she said sharply. 'There's no reason to suppose every word everyone says here is not being listened to. Not that it matters in the least. But it wouldn't take any time to secrete microphones here. Lucky we've clear consciences.'

'I see,' said Miles, rather abashed. 'I only meant . . .'

'Have you been to any good shows recently?' said Jo.

'Well, as a matter of fact, I don't go out a great deal,' said Miles. 'I find that as I get older I get more and more critical. Things that would have amused me ten years ago either bore me or irritate me now.'

'Theatre tickets are expensive,' said Jo.

'Yes, I suppose they are,' said Miles.

'I sometimes get free seats given to me,' said Jo. 'If they'd be of any use to you, I might let you have a couple from time to time.'

'That would be most kind.'

'I'll give you my address before we leave, that is, if we're ever allowed to go.'

A few minutes later a car drove up to the house and the Boss arrived. He did not always pay visits to the site, but on this occasion he felt he should do so. He sent a message to Lonsdale to announce his arrival. Lonsdale excused himself from his guests and went to see him.

'Everything all right?' asked the Boss.

'I should like to congratulate you on the efficiency of your service,' replied Lonsdale. 'It has all gone like clockwork. Not a hitch from beginning to end.'

'Delighted to hear it,' said the Boss. 'Perhaps you can recommend me to some of your friends, if they ever have any delicate matters to be attended to.'

'Well,' said Lonsdale, 'I won't promise to do that. But I'll certainly keep you in mind myself.'

'Is there anything else I can do about this?'

'I don't think so,' said Lonsdale. 'The only possible danger now is from a stray caller, but I think your people have got that pretty well taped.'

'That's splendid,' said the Boss. 'I'll go home then. Spikey knows how to get in touch with me if I'm wanted. No casualties so far, I hope?'

'None at all, thank you,' said Lonsdale.

'Good,' said the Boss. 'I hate a messy job.'

CHAPTER FOURTEEN

Direct Evidence

WHEN the hearing was resumed Charles said that he did not want to ask any further questions of Miles for the moment. Herbert Adams was the next witness. He gave similar evidence to that given by Miles, and he identified photostat copies of the newspaper he had rescued.

'You will see from these pictures,' said Broadwater, 'that the threatening letter sent to Mr Barnwell fits exactly into the spaces in the newspaper. At the trial an expert was called, who demonstrated this beyond doubt. But really an expert isn't required. If one looks at it carefully it is reasonably plain to anyone.'

'Well, Southdown,' said the judge, 'you've seen the two exhibits. Do you agree that they're an exact fit?'

'Yes,' said Charles. 'I'm prepared to admit that.'

'What about the glove?' said the judge.

'You'll see about that from the evidence of the police inspector who interviewed the accused. I gather it was not considered necessary or politic to have the inspector here today. At least I take it he isn't here?'

'No, he's not,' said Charles.

'Well,' said Broadwater, 'in that case I might as well deal with his evidence now. He said that, when he interviewed the prisoner, he produced the glove which Mr Adams had found, and asked him if he had any like it. The prisoner produced a right-hand glove but said that he had recently lost the left. It was the left glove which Mr

Adams and Mr Hampton had seen the man drop and
which Mr Adams took to the police station. No one could,
of course, say that it was the prisoner's missing glove, but
he himself admitted that it was exactly like his own. He
also admitted that he had lost it on the same day that Mr
Adams found the glove. He did say that he had not lost
it in the park but, he thought, at his club.'

'What d'you say about that, Southdown?' asked the
judge.

'It's substantially correct, Judge,' said Charles. 'Mr
Walsh did lose his glove and the one found was exactly
like the missing one. I don't admit that it was found by
Mr Adams in the way he suggests, but it may very well be
the missing glove.'

'Very well,' said the judge. 'You'd better ask Mr Adams
some questions about it. Because, if it is, your cl . . .—if it is
Walsh's glove, it seems pretty clear that he was the man
who threw away the newspaper from which the threatening letter was cut out. And if that is so . . .'

'Mr Walsh strongly denies that he threw away any
newspaper into the litter basket. But he was dressed in a
morning coat and grey top hat.'

'Then you'd better question Mr Adams about it,' said
the judge.

'What time did this happen?' was the first question.

' 'Arf past two,' said Adams.

'Why are you so certain? Had you a watch?'

'I asked this gentleman,' and he indicated Miles, 'what
time it was.'

'Why did you want to know what the time was?'

'It's important, the time is.'

'Why? You had nothing to do, had you? You were
going to wait to see if the gentleman came back for his
glove.'

'I like to know the time, see. Always 'ave. Not so
important in the day as at night, but you gets the 'abit.'

'What d'you mean—not so important in the day as at night? You're not a housebreaker by any chance?'

'No, I ain't. But my brother was, if you want to know. And 'e taught me to be careful about the time. It was important to 'im. D'you want to know why?'

'Well, why?'

'Well, it's like this 'ere. My brother didn't like being pinched, but, when they found 'im on the job, that was a fair cop.'

'What's that got to do with it?'

'I'm telling yer. What 'e didn't like was to be pinched for nothink.'

'I can understand that, but what's that got to do with noticing the time?'

'Well, it's like this 'ere. My brother might think of a job ter do while 'e was dressing 'isself in the morning. But you can't pinch a man just for thinking, can you? Well, you can't anyway. I know that much meself. It's a free country. You can think what yer like. Now, if you 'appen to be carrying a jemmy or a screwdriver or some skellington keys or somethink wot might be useful on a job, they can't pinch yer for it before nine at night, see? You can go up to a copper at half-past eight and wave them in 'is face and say "see these, chum?" and he can't do nothing to yer except tell yer to move on. Unless he can read yer thoughts, and it ain't come to that yet. But if it's arter nine o'clock 'e can pinch yer for carrying 'ousebreaking implements by night, see? And my brother didn't like that. 'E didn't see why 'e should be pinched a mile away from the job 'e was going to do, any more than 'e could be pinched while 'e was dressing 'isself in the morning. It stands to reason, don't it? 'E 'adn't done nothing wrong by carrying the things. 'E might change 'is mind on the way to the job and go 'ome. No, my brother didn't 'old with being pinched for nothing. On the job was one thing, but on the way to it was another. So 'e acted thoughtful, my brother did. 'E made up 'is mind when 'e was going to do the job, and then 'e'd take up the old instruments and 'ide 'em near the place at about 'arf past eight. So they couldn't do nothing to 'im, unless they caught 'im on the job. And that suited 'im. 'E didn't like being pinched for nothing, my brother didn't. So you see, guv, if you want to be sure you're before nine o'clock, you've got to make sure of the time. Guessing won't do. You got ter know. And, once you get used to knowing the time, you sort of always know it.'

'But this was your brother, I thought, not you?'

'Yes, but I used to have to find out the time for 'im, and that's 'ow I got into the 'abit. So that's 'ow I knew it was 'arf past three when I saw the gentleman.'

'I thought you said half-past two.'

'You got me all muddled. Yus, it was 'arf past two.'

'Sure it wasn't half-past three?'

'I just told yer. It was 'arf past two.'

'Where's your brother now?'

'Dunno.'

'Sure you had a brother?'

'Course I'm sure.'

'Just the one?'

'Yus.'

'Any sisters?'

'No.'

'When did you last see your brother?'

' 'Ow should I know?'

'What time of the day was it when you last saw him? Before or after 9 p.m.?'

'I think,' said the judge, 'we're wandering rather a long way from the subject. It's the glove you're challenging, not the time, I gather.'

'Well,' said Charles, 'we have strayed a bit, I agree, but my suggestion is that the whole of this episode has been invented, glove and all.'

'But a glove was produced,' said the judge. 'You admit that.'

'I agree,' said Charles, 'and I expect it was Mr Walsh's glove.'

'Then I don't quite see where this is getting you.'

'Suppose,' said Charles, 'this was a plot. The simple way of doing it would be to steal Mr Walsh's glove, while he was at his club or somewhere. Not very difficult for determined people.'

'You're assuming a most diabolical plot,' said the judge, 'and at the moment there is not the least evidence of it.'

'Perhaps not at the moment,' said Charles. 'Perhaps there wasn't one at all. But, if my instructions are right, there was such a plot. And, if there was, there's at least a reasonable chance we shall be able to prove it.'

'All right,' said the judge. 'Have you anything more to ask Mr Adams?'

'Not at the moment,' said Charles.

'The next witness,' said Broadwater, 'is dead, but I can read his evidence from the shorthand note. His widow is present in case my opponent wants to ask her anything.'

Broadwater then read the evidence of the late Kenneth Meadowes. He admitted that he was a man of bad character with many previous convictions. He said that he was approached by Lonsdale three days before Adolphus was killed, and asked if he could drive a car. He said he could. He was then asked if he'd do a job for Lonsdale, a job for which he would be very well paid. He asked what sort of a job it was. Lonsdale, he said, replied that it was easy enough and would only take a few seconds, adding that it meant 'driving a car and not stopping.'

'He told me,' Meadowes had sworn, 'that I was to wait round a particular corner with the engine running and that, as soon as a man whom he would identify to me walked into the road, I was to drive straight at him hard and then drive on until I was well out of the area. I was then to drive to a lonely spot in the country, to examine the car for blood or any other marks, clean it up as far as possible and do any first aid touching up necessary, and then leave it. He would arrange for it to be picked up. I did what he told me, ran over the man and drove away as he'd said and left the car in the country. I was paid £50 by the accused. I didn't take the number of the car, but it was a large blue car. It might have been a Humber. I was too taken up with the job I'd promised to do to notice much about it.'

In reply to further questions, Meadowes had said that he realised he was committing murder, and that anything he said might be used in evidence if he were charged with the murder.

'Meadowes died a few days after the trial,' said Broadwater. 'Does my friend want to ask Mrs Meadowes any questions?'

Charles said that he did.

'I'm sorry to have to ask you these questions, Mrs Meadowes,' he began. 'I hope they won't distress you too much.'

'I never wanted to come 'ere,' said Mrs Meadowes. 'I'm supposed to be getting married next week.'

'Well, I hope we'll have finished in time,' said Charles.

'Well, I hope so, really I do,' said Mrs Meadowes.

'Now, tell me, Mrs Meadowes,' said Charles, 'your husband died of cancer, didn't he?'

'Yes.'

'Which he had had for some time?'

'Yes.'

'Had he been attending hospital?'

' 'E 'ad 'ad treatment, but they said there was nothing more they could do for 'im. So they sent 'im 'ome.'

'He could still walk about?'

'Oh—'e could walk about.'

'When did he finally take to his bed?'

'About a week afore 'e died.'

'They told him at the hospital that he was a hopeless case?'

'Yes, they told 'im.'

'Is that why he went to the police and confessed?'

'I don't rightly know. I didn't know nothing about it.'

'But you knew he went to the police?'

'Oh, I knew that.'

'And when he went to the police he was a dying man?'

'Yes.'

'So he had nothing to fear from any confession he might make?'

'I don't know about that.'

'Did anyone pay him anything to go to the police?'

' 'Ow d'you mean, pay 'im anything?'

'I mean what I say. Did anyone pay him anything to go to the police?'

'I shouldn't think so.'

'Did this lady ever call on you?' and Charles pointed to Jo.

' 'Oo, 'er?'

'Yes. Did she ever call on you?'

'I don't think so.'

'You don't *think* so. Don't you know?'

'We 'ad visitors from the 'ospital.'

'But she wasn't from the hospital.'

'Oh—wasn't she?'

'Then she did call on you?'

'Not as I knows of.'

'Mrs Meadowes, I'm sorry to have to ask you this, but your husband had a dreadful character, hadn't he?'

' 'E was all right to me, when 'e wasn't in the drink.'

'If someone had wanted a man to commit perjury, they couldn't have made a better choice than your husband, could they? He was a hardened criminal and he was dying.'

'A good man to commit a murder for you,' commented Broadwater.

'Had he ever been convicted of any crimes of violence?' asked Charles.

'Only for bashing me. But 'e was in the drink then and didn't rightly know what 'e was doing.'

'So, apart from a conviction for knocking you about, he'd never been convicted for violence?'

'Not really. There was 'is mother of course, but 'e only got three months for that.'

'Well,' said Charles, 'is it fair to say that he never hit anyone, except members of his own family?'

'Yes, that's right,' said Mrs Meadowes. 'I don't know if you count me sister-in-law as family. It was when 'e was in the drink. 'E was ever so kind when 'e was sober. Unless 'e was in one of 'is moods.'

'Oh, he had moods too, did he?'

'Well, not to say moods, but it didn't do to speak to 'im when 'e was in them.'

'So, apart from his family, including sisters-in-law, whom he sometimes hit when he was in a mood or drunk, was he ever violent to anyone?'

'Not wot you'd call violent. It didn't do to argue with 'im, of course, but a lot of men are like that. 'Is brother was just the same. Didn't like a argument. Now, I like one, all friendly, if you see what I mean. But 'e didn't. 'E couldn't abear a argument. 'E didn't say much, though. But if there was something lying 'andy 'e'd use it all right. No, 'e was a good 'usband as they go, but it didn't do to argue with 'im. Least, not if 'e was in a mood or in the drink.'

'And how often was he in a mood, or drunk?'

'Week-ends mostly—and Thursdays. I 'ad my 'arf day Thursdays. So we used to go to the boozer. 'E was all right for the first four pints. But after that 'e used to turn difficult. Couldn't please 'im no 'ow. Seemed to want you to argue and, when you did, 'e bashed you. But 'e didn't mean any 'arm. Didn't know 'is own strength.'

'I hope your new husband will be gentler,' said the judge.

' 'E'd better be,' said Mrs Meadowes. ' 'E only comes up to 'ere,' and she indicated her shoulder. 'I chose 'im special,' she added. 'Laid 'im flat a week ago, if yer want ter know. Not taking any chances this time. But 'e wasn't a bad man, my Kennie, not to say bad. I known plenty worse. It takes all sorts, don't it?'

'I'd just like to get this clear, Mrs Meadowes,' said Charles. 'Your husband was violent to his family and when he was drunk or in a mood, but not otherwise?'

'Only to the police,' said Mrs Meadowes. ' 'E didn't 'old with them.'

CHAPTER FIFTEEN

The Stable Doorkeeper

WHILE Mrs Meadowes was being cross-examined by Charles, Colonel Pudsey-Pease, the governor of Northwall prison, was investigating Lonsdale's escape. The governor was a man who was never at a loss for a word. As far as quantity was concerned, he was a born small-talker. Some people dread cocktail parties. 'What shall I talk about?' plaintively asks the wife of the husband or the husband of the wife, as the case may be. Colonel Pudsey-Pease never had to ask such a question. He was equally at home with his convicts, his warders and the ladies and gentlemen at the Lord-Lieutenant's garden party.

He would have chatted cheerfully to the Prime Minister about Britain's policy in the Far East or the problems of inflation, about which subjects he knew practically nothing. He once met a distinguished author of fiction. Almost immediately he said: 'I've got a plot for you.'

Wearily the author looked, not too obviously, for escape to some other part of the room, but, finding none, he said as politely as possible: 'Oh, really?'

'Yes, this should interest you,' the Colonel went on enthusiastically. 'There's a woman in my mother-in-law's road who only goes out on Thursdays. At least they've never seen her out on any other day. They call her "Mrs Thursday." And what d'you think her real name is?'

'Mundy?' ventured the distinguished author, who was

125

fast becoming as distinguished for his good manners as for his good books.

'No,' said the Colonel. 'Thursby. You could do something with that, I fancy. It's all yours. No charge.'

'That's most kind,' said the author, 'but you really ought to use it yourself. I'm sure you'd do much better with it than I should.'

'Well, I don't really write,' said the Colonel. 'Just a few scribblings. Not that I haven't had a lot to write about. Some of the fellows under my care are a book in themselves. Had a chap the other day who couldn't read or write. What d'you think he was in for?'

'Bigamy,' suggested the author. 'You don't require the G.C.E. for that.'

'Forgery,' said the Colonel. 'Would you believe it? Couldn't read a word, couldn't write a word. But, when it came to mere imitation of someone else's writing, he took a lot of beating. And bank-notes! I'd have fallen for them. Brilliant fellow. Such a pity. And some of the confidence tricksters I've had. You wouldn't believe some of the things they've done. Mark you, the public's gullible— and greedy. Or they wouldn't fall for it. But he thought up some pretty artful ones, I can tell you. Nearly fooled me once, but I just remembered in time who I was talking to.'

The Colonel would have been equally at ease discussing education with the headmaster of a public school, law with a judge or ballet with Ninette de Valois.

But he was very worried by Lonsdale's escape.

'I'm determined to get to the bottom of this,' he said to his new deputy. 'When a man escapes, somebody in the prison knows where he's making for and I'm going to find out—if I have to put them all on bread and water.'

He had not the slightest intention of acting in this illegal manner, but he wanted to show how strongly he felt on the subject.

'We've got to get this fellow back,' he said. 'There've been too many of these escapes. And the trouble is, unless the fellow's dangerous, the public don't want him to be caught. Sentimental idiots. But just let them think that the wanted man might bump them off and they'll howl their heads off at the wicked prison authorities for not keeping him inside. I tell you, Maitland,' he went on, 'if you took a Gallup poll today, to find out how many people wanted Walsh caught, you'd find ninety per cent against it. But if we published that, since coming to prison he'd become dangerous, had knocked out two warders, half-killed a third and was believed to be carrying a revolver, it would be the other way round quick enough. Blithering lot of idiots. They're only sentimental when they're not afraid for their own skins.'

'I quite agree with you,' said Maitland. 'Who are you going to see first?'

'Well, the fellow we really want to see is a chap who was released not long before Walsh escaped. He shared a cell with him. Spikey they called him. I've told the police about him, but apparently they can't find him at the moment. So I think I'll see Jimmy Simpson first. If there's any mischief going on, he'll know about it.'

So Simpson was brought before the governor. He was offered a seat.

'Let me see,' said the governor, 'how much longer have you got?'

'You should know, sir,' said Simpson, 'better than me.'

'Come now,' said the governor, 'don't be foolish. Politeness costs nothing, but impertinence can be expensive here.'

Simpson said nothing.

'Another five years, isn't it?'

Simpson still said nothing.

The chief warder was about to tell Simpson to answer, when the governor held up his hand.

'The other day,' he said, 'the Home Secretary ordered

the immediate release of a man who had still five years to go. Why d'you think he did that, Simpson?'

'Ask him, sir,' said Simpson.

'You——' began the warder.

'That's all right,' said the governor. 'I understand. We understand one another, don't we, Simpson? You think I'm going to ask you for information and that I'm hinting that you might get some remission if you gave it to me, not promising, mind you, but hinting. That's what you think, isn't it, Simpson?'

'I don't think anything at all, sir.'

'And you don't think it's right to split on your pals. That's it, isn't it? Well, think it over, Simpson. Five years is a long time. All right, you can take him away.'

As soon as they were alone, the governor said:

'Gently does it, you see, Maitland. I've had that type before. He's got plenty of time to think about what I've said. I believe in sowing the seed. But don't force it. Now let's see Everton.'

Everton was of a very different type and was not offered a seat. He would have talked as much as the governor, if given a chance.

'You won't tell anyone if I tell you, sir, will you? Because, if you did, I'd be for it.'

'You will be fully protected, Everton.'

'Well then, sir, I can tell you where you'll find him. Ireland. That's where he is. He was going to lie low in London for a few days, and then off to Ireland.'

'Whereabouts in Ireland? It's quite a large place.'

'Well, of course, he may have moved, but he was starting in Dublin.'

'Any kind of address?'

'Oh no, sir. Don't suppose he knew it himself, sir.'

'And what was he going to do in Ireland? Any idea?'

'Now you have me, sir. Lie low, I suppose. He didn't need to work.'

'So you think that, if we look for someone lying low in Ireland, we might find him.'

'I was only trying to help, sir.'

'Then who told you all this?'

'Just prison gossip, sir.'

'Very well, thank you, Everton, you may go.'

Methodically the governor interviewed every prisoner who might have known something.

'I don't have to answer, do I, sir?' asked one. 'I don't lose marks if I refuse?'

'No,' said the governor, 'you don't have to answer.'

'Then what'll I get if I do tell you something, sir?'

'I can make no promises.'

'Well, what's the inducement, sir?'

'The inducement,' said the governor, 'is the possibility —only possibility, mind you—of remission if you give me really useful information.'

'Possibility isn't much, sir. Would you make it probability?'

'I can't make it anything. You know perfectly well I've no power to do so. I can only tell the Home Secretary that you've been of use—if you have been. It's entirely up to him then.'

'What are the chances, sir?'

'I simply can't tell you, but, if what you tell me does really help, I'll certainly do what I can for you. I can't say more than that, and you'll have no right to complain if you get nothing out of it.'

'Very well, sir, I'll take a chance. I think you'll find he's staying with one of the judges.'

'What!'

'That's what I heard, sir. He's going to stay with a judge. No one will look for him there.'

'Don't be ridiculous. Take this man away,' said the governor. He had had a fruitless day, and he was really angry.

E

CHAPTER SIXTEEN

A Different Light

'Look, Bert,' said Bert's young woman. 'Look what I've found,' and she showed him the piece of paper which had got stuck on the hedge. 'D'you think it's real?'

'Send the police to Howard House,' read Bert aloud. 'It's a joke, I expect. That's where his nibs lives. What'd he want with the police? Give us a kiss.'

She obliged.

'No, a proper one.'

She obliged again.

'But suppose it was real, Bert,' she said. 'Shouldn't we take it to the station?'

'Well,' said Bert, 'it wouldn't do any harm, I suppose. But there's no need to hurry ourselves. I like it here.'

'So do I, Bert.'

'We'll take it in when we go home then. That'll suit everybody.'

And Bert turned his attention again to what to him and his young woman on their half-day off were more important matters.

Meanwhile Charles, having finished for the moment his cross-examination of Mrs Meadowes, was inviting the judge to look at the evidence which had so far been tendered.

'All I can say,' said the judge, 'is that I can see no reason for disagreeing with the jury's verdict. It is

perfectly true that the most important witness is dead, and
was a man of bad character, but he did say on oath that
he killed the dead man and was paid to kill him by the
convicted man. Now it's obvious, I should have thought,
that Meadowes had no personal reason for killing Mr
Barnwell. Indeed, as far as I know, the only person who
would have benefited from his death is your . . . is the
convicted man. Well, now, of course, it's possible that
Meadowes told a cock and bull story and was paid to do
so. But there's no evidence of that at all. It's true that it is
unusual for a man to confess to a murder in this particular
way. But it would be equally unusual for a man to commit
perjury in this particular way. Obviously the jury had to
be warned that Meadowes was an accomplice and that
his evidence ought not to be accepted without corroboration, but, of course, they were so warned. And now look
at the corroboration. There was abundant evidence not
only that your . . . that Walsh benefited by the killing
of Mr Barnwell, but that he had sent the threatening
letter and the road sign. Well, now, if the jury accepted
that evidence, and I see no reason why they should not
have done so, the position is that the convicted man
threatened the deceased with unpleasant consequences if
he didn't discontinue his action for slander, that the
deceased continued with his action, that he was thereupon run over and killed, and the man who killed him
said the convicted man paid him to do it. That was the
evidence at the trial. What more do you want? As far as I
can see, it was a perfectly proper conviction. Your suggestion is that the whole thing was a fake. I can only say
that, at the moment, there is no evidence of that whatever.'

'I quite understand your present views, Judge,' said
Charles. 'I propose to call Mr Walsh to see if he can change
them.'

Lonsdale went to the witness chair and sat down. He
described his financial affairs, in so far as they were

relevant to the dispute with Adolphus Barnwell. He
referred to the slander action and admitted that it was a
grave annoyance to him.

'I go further than that,' he said. 'My solicitor told me
that, unless Mr Barnwell died, the slander action would
continue. I thereupon wished Mr Barnwell dead.'

'And he died,' put in Broadwater.

'And I agree,' went on Lonsdale, 'that, before he died,
I sent that threatening letter and the road sign. But I
didn't throw the newspaper into a litter basket in the
park. I burned it in a grate in my house.'

Jo, who had been looking more and more triumphant
as she saw the complete failure of Lonsdale's plan, could
not resist a cry of triumph.

'I knew it,' she said. 'I knew it.'

The effect upon the judge of this uncontrollable outburst was remarkable. He turned towards Jo and asked
immediately:

'What did you know, Madam?'

'You heard him yourself, Sir George,' said Jo. 'You
heard him admit sending the letter and burning the
newspaper in his grate. He's admitted it.'

For the first time since the enquiry had begun, the
judge began to take a real interest in the proceedings. Up
till that moment he had listened to the evidence and considered everything put before him with a fairly strong
preconceived idea that there was nothing in it at all.
Lonsdale appeared to him to be one of those self-righteous
megalomaniacs who, though obviously guilty, almost
think themselves into believing in their own innocence. In
the judge's experience he would certainly not have been
the first plainly guilty man who protested his innocence
throughout his life. As the judge was compelled to inves-
tigate the trial, he had done so with reasonable care and,
indeed, his judicial training had compelled him to conduct
the proceedings as though he really wanted to enquire

into the matter. But, until Jo's outburst, he had had no idea at all that there might be something in Lonsdale's allegation that he had been framed. He was glad that it was not a formal trial and that he could turn his attention to Jo at once.

'Mrs Barnwell,' he said slowly, 'why was it a surprise to you that the witness admitted sending the letter? You knew he'd sent it. You'd heard all the evidence.'

'I never thought he'd admit it,' said Jo.

'But he didn't admit the evidence given against him. He said that he burned the newspaper in his own grate. Whereupon you said: "I knew it, I knew it." And you said it in a tone of obvious delight.'

'Of course I was pleased,' said Jo. 'I want this man back in prison.'

'That you have made clear enough,' said the judge, 'but was not your pleasure at your *guess* that he sent the letter being right?'

The judge looked hard at Jo as he asked this question, and she could not continue to look at him. Nor could she immediately answer the judge's question.

'Now, Mrs Barnwell,' he went on, 'if what the convicted man says is true, those two witnesses who told this elaborate story about the park are telling lies. And there could be no possible reason for their telling lies unless they had been paid to do so. Of that there can be no doubt. So, if he burned the newspaper in his grate, someone persuaded those two men to put up their story. And someone cut out a newspaper so as to fit the letter which was in your possession.'

The judge paused and then added:

'And I suppose someone could quite easily have stolen his glove first.'

The whole atmosphere in the room had changed and everyone waited for the judge's next words.

'Mrs Barnwell,' he said, 'can you suggest anyone except

yourself who might have persuaded those men to tell this story?'

'I certainly didn't,' said Jo.

'I didn't ask you that,' said the judge. 'Can you suggest anyone else who might have done so?'

'No,' said Jo, 'and I don't know why you should assume that they're not telling the truth.'

'It was you, madam, who first did that,' said the judge, 'when you said "I knew it" on hearing the witness say that he had burned the newspaper in his grate—the newspaper which was produced in court.'

'Does it matter how he did it?' said Jo. 'He sent the letter all right.'

'We shall see if it matters,' said the judge. 'I can imagine it mattering a great deal. Well, we'd better continue with your story, Mr Walsh.'

Lonsdale was not the only one to notice the 'Mr.'

'Tell me, Mr Walsh,' said Charles. 'Did you ever ask Meadowes to run over Mr Barnwell?'

'I did not,' said Lonsdale.

'Had you in fact ever seen Meadowes before you saw him in Court?'

'To the best of my belief I had never seen him before.'

As soon as he had said that, Jo started to look feverishly in her bag. After a short search she obviously found something in it which pleased and surprised her. She at once got up and went across to Broadwater and whispered to him. Meanwhile Charles was still cross-examining.

'Did you attend a wedding one day in Bayswater?' he asked Lonsdale.

'Yes, I did, and Mrs Barnwell knew that I did. She also knew that it was at a church near to Hyde Park, and that I might easily have taken a stroll in the park before or after the ceremony. I probably did.'

'What about your glove? Did you lose it in the park?'

'I did not. I first missed it in my club. That was before I went to the wedding. I had not been near the park at that time. When I missed it I assumed that I had dropped it in the street and, of course, I may have. But now I believe it was probably stolen from the cloakroom in my club. It would be easy enough for a stranger to appear to walk in with a member. Indeed, for all I know, the thief walked in with me.'

'What about the road sign?'

'Yes, I sent that too. I wanted to scare him. I may add that I sent appropriate compensation to the Council to whom it belonged.'

'There's only one other thing I want to ask you,' said Charles. 'Why didn't you give evidence at your trial?'

'I wanted to, but my counsel was very frightened of the effect of the admissions I should have to make about the threatening letter and road sign. And he persuaded me not to. I can't pretend that I tried very hard to alter his view. If you employ an expert, you take his advice. He told me that it was safer to rely on the fact that Meadowes was not only a party to the crime on his own confession, but had a very bad record as well.'

'Thank you,' said Charles. 'That is all I wish to ask.'

Broadwater then started to cross-examine.

'I think you said that you'd never seen Meadowes before you saw him at the Magistrate's Court?'

'That is correct.'

'You're sure of that?'

'Certainly, so far as I know.'

Broadwater handed him a photograph which he half covered over.

'Is that a picture of you?' he asked.

'Yes,' said Lonsdale. 'Not a very good one, but it's me all right.'

Broadwater then showed him the rest of the photograph.

'And who are you talking to?' he asked.

'Good God!' said Lonsdale. 'Some people are never satisfied.'

'What on earth do you mean?' asked the judge.

'I mean this,' said Lonsdale, 'and, if anything will convince you of this woman's dishonesty, this will. This is a picture of me talking to the late Kenneth Meadowes.'

'I thought you said you'd never seen him before?' said the judge.

'I did,' said Lonsdale, 'and I meant it. And, in the sense I said it, it was true. I said I had never seen him before, as far as I knew. But, of course, one has seen all sorts of people in trains and in the street and in theatres and so on. And one doesn't remember them, any more than one remembers the man who stops you and asks for a light or to know the way. But people do ask for lights and do ask you the way. And I cannot tell you what Kenneth Meadowes was asking me when that photograph was taken. But I can say that I had never seen him before then—in the same sense as I've just mentioned—and I can say that I was not then asking him to murder Mr Barnwell; and I can say that it is very, very extraordinary that someone should have thought it worth taking a photograph of the two of us, and even more extraordinary that the photograph should be in the possession of that woman.'

'Yes,' said the judge, 'but there is something even more important than that. Why was this not produced at the trial? You were in the case, Broadwater. Do you know why?'

'Very simply,' said Broadwater, 'because the prosecution had no idea of its existence.'

'I see,' said the judge. 'Why didn't you give it to the police at that time, Mrs Barnwell?'

'I didn't think it important. I don't know why I've kept it so long. I only looked in my bag on the off-chance.'

'You didn't think it important,' said the judge, heavily underlining the words.

At that moment one of the guards came in hastily and spoke to Lonsdale. He thought for a moment and then said:

'Sir George, there's a police car coming up the drive. A real one, I mean.'

'I see,' said the judge, and he, too, thought for a moment. As a judge and a lawyer he knew that, from the point of view of arriving at the truth in Lonsdale's case, it was vitally important that he should go on with the enquiry without interruption. Although he could, no doubt, ensure that a further enquiry would be held later, the witnesses would have had time to think by then. If, as he was now beginning to believe, Lonsdale's complaint that he had been framed was justified, now was the psychological moment to go on with the investigation. Any serious delay might be fatal to the ascertainment of the truth.

'May I be allowed to go and interview the police myself?' he asked.

'Yes, Sir George,' said Lonsdale without hesitation.

The judge got up and went to the front door. The car had just arrived. An inspector and sergeant got out.

'I'm so sorry to trouble you, my Lord,' began the inspector, 'but we've just had this brought in to the police station. I thought I'd better come down myself.'

The inspector handed to the judge the note which Bert and his young lady had found.

The judge laughed.

'Well, it's nice of you to come, Inspector. I'll let you know if I want you. Good afternoon. Forgive my rushing off, but I'm just in the middle of something.'

The judge went in.

The inspector looked puzzled.

'Extraordinary old boy,' he said to the sergeant. 'Didn't want to know what it was all about or anything. Practical joke, I suppose. Oh well—off we go.'

As they drove off, the inspector said to the sergeant:

'What's one of our chaps doing up here?'

'We haven't got one,' said the sergeant.

'Well, I'm sure I saw one going round the house as we drove up. Seemed to be in a hurry.'

'Must have been a mistake, inspector,' said the sergeant. 'There's no one up here.'

'It's all very odd,' said the inspector, 'I could have sworn I saw one.'

'Helmet or cap?' asked the sergeant.

'Helmet,' said the inspector.

'Perhaps the judge is playing charades, inspector,' suggested the sergeant.

'From the way he behaved he might be playing anything,' said the inspector. 'Now what on earth are we going to put in the report book? Don't want to be had up for contempt of Court. It'll take a bit of thinking out. Any bright ideas?'

'I'd be an inspector if I had any,' said the sergeant.

The judge had meanwhile hurried back to the enquiry. There was a very different atmosphere prevailing. Lonsdale was full of expectancy. Jo was extremely worried but was grimly determined to battle on. The other witnesses were only dimly aware of what was happening or what might be in store for them.

'Now, Mrs Barnwell,' said the judge briskly, as soon as he had returned, 'you had this photograph in your possession at the time of Mr Walsh's trial, but you didn't think it important enough to show to the police. Is that the truth?'

'Yes,' said Jo.

'Did you expect the accused to plead guilty or not guilty to the charge?'

'Not guilty, I suppose.'

'Did you expect him to deny his guilt in the witness box?'

'He didn't go into the witness box.'

'You didn't know that he wasn't going to give evidence, did you?'

'No.'

'Then, before the trial started, you must have thought it at least possible that he would go into the witness box?'

'I'm not sure that I thought about it at all.'

'Are you saying that, before the trial, you never visualised the man you believed to have murdered your husband, and whom you accordingly and very naturally hated, going into the witness box and telling his story? Surely you must have thought about it? You're an intelligent woman.'

'Thank you,' said Jo, 'but I'm not a judge or even a lawyer. And we think about things differently from lawyers. You always think about things in terms of witnesses and evidence and so forth. Ordinary folk are different.'

'I dare say, Mrs Barnwell,' said the judge, 'but ordinary folk like you have their passions and one of the things you wanted was to see the man you believed to have murdered your husband brought to justice. That at least is right, isn't it?'

'Yes, that is right,' said Jo. 'And he was. He was brought to justice. He was found guilty—as he was.'

'I am beginning to have grave doubts,' said the judge, 'if he was brought to justice. He was tried, certainly, but the question of justice is another matter. Whether or not you considered the possibility of the accused giving evidence, you surely must have realised the possibility that he would deny having asked Meadowes to run over your husband?'

'I tell you, I never thought about it. I told the police all I knew, and there it ended.'

'Might I interpose a question, Judge?' said Charles.

'What is it?' asked the judge.

'Well, Judge, she was at the Magistrate's Court, and must have heard the police officer, who interviewed Mr Walsh, give evidence that he denied ever having spoken to Meadowes.'

'Yes,' said the judge, 'thank you. Well, Mrs Barnwell, you heard what Mr Southdown said. It's right, isn't it? You knew before the trial at the Old Bailey that the prisoner was denying ever having spoken to Meadowes?'

'It's a long time ago now,' said Jo, 'but I suppose I heard it.'

'Then why on earth did you not at once produce this photograph and prove that his denial was false?'

Jo did not answer at once.

'Here was this man who had murdered your husband calmly saying that he had never seen or spoken to the man who actually did the murder. And here were you with a trump card in your possession. Why did you not produce it?'

'I can't really say,' said Jo. 'I didn't, that's all.'

'Where had you got this photograph from, madam?' asked the judge.

'I'm not sure. I think Mrs Meadowes gave it to me,' said Jo.

The judge immediately turned to Mrs Meadowes.

'Is that right?' he asked, 'did you give this to Mrs Barnwell?'

Mrs Meadowes looked blankly at the photograph.

'That's 'im,' she said.

'Yes, we all know it's your late husband,' said the judge, 'but have you ever seen this photograph before in your life?'

'I couldn't rightly say,' said Mrs Meadowes, 'but I'd know 'im anywhere. 'E was a 'andsome man, until the drink got 'im. But I've known worse nor 'im,' she added. 'And sober, too.'

'No doubt,' said the judge, 'but you don't remember ever giving this photograph to Mrs Barnwell, do you?'

'It wasn't the one on the mantelpiece. I wouldn't 'ave given 'er that. That was took on our wedding day.'

'Quite so,' said the judge.

'I'm keeping it there when I'm married again.'

'Yes, yes,' said the judge impatiently.

'That's all arranged. 'E didn't take to the idea at first, but 'e liked the frame. So that's settled,' said Mrs Meadowes happily.

'But this photograph was never in a frame, was it?'

'I never sold it, straight I didn't. 'E did all that sort of thing 'isself.'

'Mrs Meadowes,' said the judge, 'will you please try to follow what I'm asking you. Have you ever seen this photograph before?'

Mrs Meadowes looked at the photograph critically.

' 'Ave I ever seen it before?' she asked.

'Yes, have you?'

'Where?'

'Anywhere.'

'Ask 'er,' and Mrs Meadowes pointed to Jo, adding, ' 'ave I ever seen it before?'

'You know you gave it to me,' said Jo.

'That's right,' said Mrs Meadowes.

'Please don't interrupt,' said the judge.

'Why shouldn't I?' said Jo. 'This seems to be a free for all, with the police being sent away and everything.'

'That's my responsibility,' said the judge.

'I'll see that it is,' said Jo. 'Here am I, an ordinary citizen, kidnapped by a lot of thugs and, when I have the chance of being freed by the police, a High Court judge prevents it.'

'We'll deal with one thing at a time,' said the judge evenly. 'You can make any complaint you like later.'

'You can be sure of that,' said Jo. 'It's outrageous.'

'I'm not going to let your threats deter me from investigating what I believe may have been a grave miscarriage of justice,' said the judge.

'It was nothing of the kind,' said Jo.

'Mrs Meadowes,' said the judge, 'I suppose you couldn't tell me who took the photograph?'

'That I couldn't,' said Mrs Meadowes, 'but it's 'im all right. There weren't two of 'im. There aren't any of 'im now, but it takes all sorts, don't it?'

'Mrs Barnwell,' said the judge, 'when do you say Mrs Meadowes gave you this photograph?'

'It's too long ago—I couldn't say.'

'And how did you happen to be seeing her?'

'I was sorry for her. I bore her no ill will. I knew her husband was dying, and I'd lost mine. There was a sort of bond between us.'

'Did you by any chance make enquiries at the hospital which he attended?' asked the judge.

'What d'you mean, make enquiries?' asked Jo.

'I mean "make enquiries." Did you make enquiries to find out how long Meadowes was likely to live? It may be possible to check that, you know.'

'I may have at some time.'

'Did you know that Meadowes had a very bad criminal record?'

'Of course I did at one stage.'

'Did you arrange for him to approach Mr Walsh in the street, and to have a photograph—this photograph—taken?'

'Of course not. It's ridiculous.'

'And did you keep the photograph in reserve for use if necessary?'

'Absurd. Why should I want to do that? If I'd had it taken specially, I would have produced it, wouldn't I? That's what you suggested yourself.'

'I asked you why you didn't produce it, and you've not

given any satisfactory answer about that yet. Let me suggest a possible reason. Perhaps you thought that, if you added that piece of evidence, it might make the case too good to be true?'

'Nonsense.'

'Let us just see,' said the judge, 'and I warn you, Mr Hampton, and you, Mr Adams, to listen carefully to what I'm going to say. Mrs Barnwell felt sure that Mr Walsh had murdered her husband. But she had no evidence of any kind that he had done so. She had a threatening letter, which she felt sure he had written. And that was all. Now, I'm going to suggest what she might have done. I am not saying at present that she did it, but just that she might have done it. She makes enquiries to find out the name of a hardened criminal who is suffering from a fatal disease. That would not be difficult to ascertain under the guise of charity. She persuaded him, under promise of a payment of money either to him or his wife or both, to go to the police and make the statement which he in fact made. But, first of all, she arranges for the photograph to be taken. She then arranges for someone to steal Mr Walsh's glove. She next finds two characters who are prepared to commit perjury for money. She has the original threatening letter and cuts out a newspaper so that it will marry up with the letter. Now that may not be exactly what happened, it may not be what happened at all, but, if it did, it would account for the whole of this evidence, would it not? Can you suggest any flaw in my reasoning, Mrs Barnwell?'

'If you choose to assume that everyone's committed perjury, I can't stop you,' said Jo. 'But you could say the same in any case.'

'In other cases you don't find photographs withheld by a witness for the prosecution, nor do you find such a witness giving that extraordinary exhibition which you gave when Mr Walsh admitted sending the threatening letter.

Which reminds me. Tell me, Mr Walsh, what did you intend by that letter?'

'I intended that Mr Barnwell should fear for his life. I wanted to frighten him out of his wits, so that he should not go on with the slander action. I do not seek to justify my action, but that is what I intended.'

'It's a great pity you didn't give evidence at your trial,' said the judge. 'I should have thought your frankness, as compared with the hedging and show of indignation by Mrs Barnwell, would have stood you in good stead with the jury.'

'It is a great pity,' said Lonsdale, 'but, as I said, I had to abide by the advice given to me.'

'And do you still say that, apart from being asked for a match or something of the sort, you had never spoken to Meadowes in your life?'

'I do,' said Lonsdale. 'Mrs Barnwell knows me well, and she knows that I never lie.'

'I know nothing of the kind,' said Jo. 'He's a liar and a humbug.'

Lonsdale went very red in the face. He must have realised that everyone was looking at him.

'I'm sorry, Sir George,' he said, 'but I find it difficult to contain myself when such a deliberate untruth is told. Mrs Barnwell knows as well as anyone that I have never told her a lie in my life.'

'Do you still say that you never—either by letter or telephone or face to face or through a third party— requested Meadowes to run over Mr Barnwell?'

'I do. The whole story is a concoction from beginning to end.'

'Very well,' said the judge. 'I think the time has now come to ask Mr Hampton some more questions.'

Miles had now begun to realise what was happening.

'As a matter of fact, I was going to ask if I could be excused. I don't feel terribly well.'

'What's the matter?' asked the judge sharply.

'I just don't feel very well.'

'In what way?'

'Don't bully the man,' said Jo. 'He said he feels ill. Have you never felt ill? You don't have to have a pain or a temperature to feel ill.'

'You seem a little anxious that he shouldn't be questioned, Mrs Barnwell. Why?' asked the judge.

'I'm nothing of the kind. You just twist everything I say. I wonder they made you a judge. You won't be one much longer after I get out of this. It's an absolute scandal. I think I'm going.'

And Jo got up to go out of the room.

'I'm sorry, Jo,' said Lonsdale, 'you're not leaving here until this is over.'

'You'll be sorry for this,' said Jo. 'You're all going to be sorry for this.'

She went back to her seat.

'What about Mr Adams?' asked the judge. 'Is he feeling quite well?'

'I'm all right,' said Mr Adams.

'Good,' said the judge. 'Tell me, Mr Adams,' he went on, 'do you know what is meant by perjury?'

'Not exactly.'

'It's telling lies on oath.'

'Oh,' said Mr Adams, 'that's bad.'

'Have you ever done it?' asked the judge.

'Wot me?' said Mr Adams, with a reasonable show of astonishment.

'Yes, you,' said the judge.

'Wot should I want ter do that for?'

'Money.'

'Oh.'

'What does that mean?' asked the judge. 'Why did you say "oh"?'

'I dunno. I just said it. It's all right, ain't it?'

'Have you ever been given money for telling lies?'

'That's asking something, ain't it?'

'I know it is. And what's the answer?'

'That'd be telling, wouldn't it?'

'Yes,' said the judge, 'and I want you to tell me.'

'Oh,' said Mr Adams.

'Well,' persisted the judge, 'when were you offered or given money to tell lies?'

'What'll 'appen to me if I tell?'

'Nothing,' said the judge. 'Nothing that anyone says at this enquiry can be used in evidence against him—or her—as the statements will have been made under duress.'

'What does all that mean?' asked Mr Adams.

'It means you can't get into trouble for what you say here.'

'Oh,' said Mr Adams. After a pause, he went on:

'But what about what I said any other time?'

'What you say now can't be used in evidence against you.'

'Why should it be?'

'It can't be.'

'Oh.'

'Well, now, Mr Adams, tell me the last time you told lies for money.'

'The last time?'

'Yes.'

'I don't rightly remember. I can tell you the time before, though.'

'What! Has it happened so often?'

'Has what happened often?'

'Have you told lies for money so often?'

'Not to say lies. I did 'elp my brother once or twice.'

'How did you help him?'

'With the time like.'

'The time?'

'Yes. I said 'e was at 'ome.'

'And he wasn't?'

' 'E might 'ave been. I was asleep.'

'So it comes to this, that you used to give your brother an alibi every now and then?'

'That's right. But I stopped it in the end.'

'Why was that?'

'They didn't ever believe me.'

'You must have found it a refreshing change to be believed at Mr Walsh's trial?'

'Wot's that?'

'The jury believed you about the glove and the paper.'

'Oh.'

'D'you think they should have?'

' 'Ow should I know? That's their job, ain't it?'

'But you know if you were telling the truth.'

'It ain't so easy as that. I once said my brother was in bed at 'ome all night and 'e was. You could 'ave knocked me down.'

'They believed you that time then?'

'They didn't 'ave to. 'E'd 'ad the doctor in the night, but I didn't know. I wasn't there. They let 'im go that time, though. Stands to reason. 'E'd 'ad the doctor. It was someone else, as a matter of fact.'

'Not you by any chance?' asked the judge.

'They never found 'oo it was,' said Mr Adams, 'but it weren't my brother. 'E'd 'ad the doctor.'

'Did you tell the truth about the glove and the newspaper? Did you really see anyone drop a glove and throw a newspaper in the litter basket?'

'Wot would 'appen if I said I didn't?'

'Well, for one thing, Mr Walsh would probably be let out of prison.'

' 'E's out now, ain't 'e?'

'He'd be let out properly, through the gate, not over the wall.'

'And wot about 'er. Would she go in instead?'

'No,' said the judge. 'I doubt if anything could be done to any of you.'

'So nothing can't 'appen to me whatever I say?'

'Nothing.'

'All right,' said Mr Adams. 'I'm ready. What's the question?'

'Is what you said at the trial true?'

'Nothing can't 'appen to me?'

'No.'

'Right. Well,' began Mr Adams, 'I don't feel all that good. Feel queer like.'

'Was the evidence you gave at the trial true?'

'Near enough.'

'Near enough to what?'

'Well mostly.'

'What wasn't true?'

'It was near enough.'

'You leave it to me to say if it was near enough. How much of it wasn't true? Did you ever sit in the park at all next to Mr Hampton?'

'Oh, yes, I sat next to 'im all right.'

'And did a gentleman come along and drop a glove?'

'Oh, yes, 'e did that all right.'

'And put a newspaper in the litter basket?'

'Oh, yes, I saw 'im.'

'And you went and took it out?'

'Yes.'

'And picked up the glove?'

'Yes.'

'And later took it and the newspaper to the police?'

'Yes.'

'Well, everything you said at the trial was true then?'

'I said near enough.'

'You said it was a gentleman like that one there. Was it?'

'It was about 'is heighth.'

'But you wouldn't say it was him?'

'No, I couldn't say that.'

Charles then intervened.

'Might I make a suggestion, Judge? If my case is right, this was an elaborate plot and it would be much easier for these witnesses to give evidence, if the thing really took place as far as possible. There was nothing to stop Mrs Barnwell from arranging for these men to be on a bench in the park, and from sending someone of Mr Walsh's height, dressed in a morning coat and grey top-hat, armed with Mr Walsh's glove and the cut-out newspaper. It's much easier for witnesses to give evidence of something that really happened than to have to invent it.'

'Yes, I see,' said the judge. 'And that would fit in with Mr Adams' answers "near enough." But they'd have to be primed as to what was going to happen and what they must do afterwards, or it might all go wrong. So, if it was a fake, they'd have to be a party to it.'

'Yes, Judge, I think so,' said Charles. 'Perhaps you might care to ask them about it—if they're well enough?'

'Well, Mr Hampton,' said the judge, 'I don't know if you heard what Mr Southdown said—but was the whole thing a play in which you'd agreed to take part?'

'Well,' began Miles.

'The man's not well,' said Jo, 'leave him alone.'

At first when Jo had started to behave like this everyone had been very startled. Although the judge was not in robes and the room was not a Court, everyone knew he was a judge and the idea that he could be spoken to with impunity as Jo was speaking to him had not occurred to anyone. Nor did anyone else feel like trying it. But Jo proposed to use every weapon at her disposal.

'I don't believe there's anything the matter with him,' said the judge.

'You're not a doctor, not even a bad one—you're supposed to be a judge, though no one would guess it.'

'Mrs Barnwell,' said the judge, 'when this enquiry first

started and when it appeared to me that Mr Walsh had been properly found guilty, you behaved yourself perfectly, just as though this were a Court. Do you not realise what a bad impression your altered behaviour is bound to make upon me? Don't you realise that it is likely to confirm my belief that you were party to a grave conspiracy?'

'That's no more than what I should have expected,' said Jo. 'As long as everyone licks your boots and says "Yes, my Lord" and "No, my Lord" they've got a splendid case. But, as soon as they speak their mind or hurt your dignity, you say they're guilty of conspiracy. I'm sorry for the people who have their cases tried by you.'

'Mr Hampton, do you feel well enough to answer a few questions?' asked the judge.

Miles hesitated.

'It rather depends on the questions,' he said eventually.

'I see,' said the judge. 'It's that sort of illness.'

'That's right,' said Jo, 'twist everything he says.'

'Well, then, Mr Hampton,' went on the judge, ignoring Jo, 'try this one. Before you went to sit in the park did you know that someone was going to come along and drop a glove and put a newspaper in the litter basket?'

'Well, I had an idea,' said Miles apologetically.

'And who gave you that idea?'

'It's rather a long time ago.'

'Yes, I know. But it must have been rather an unusual occurrence for you to go and sit in the park and wait for something which you knew was going to happen?'

'Yes, it was unusual,' conceded Miles.

'Then you should be able to tell me who asked you to do it. Such a thing has presumably never happened to you before or since?'

'I can't say that it has.'

'Well, then, can't you help me? Was it a man or a woman?'

'It's a little difficult.'

'It must have been one or the other.'

'Yes, I suppose so.'

'Then which was it? Come, Mr Hampton, I'm sure you want to help me.'

'The velvet glove,' sneered Jo. 'Come along, my dear little man, no one's going to hurt you. Just say what I want you to say and then you may go. It's lucky everyone doesn't know how judges behave.'

'Well, Mr Hampton,' said the judge, 'a man or a woman?'

'I really don't feel terribly well,' said Miles.

'You're quite well enough to answer that question.'

'I'm going to faint,' said Miles—and fainted.

'Well done,' said Jo. 'Now you can hit him on the head. He won't feel it.'

Miles was soon restored with a little cold water and, while he was resting, the judge questioned Adams again.

'Well, Mr Adams, did you know it was all going to happen and, if so, who told you?'

'Well, it was like this 'ere,' said Adams. 'A bloke came to me and asked if I'd like to make a bit. Naturally I wanted to know what it was all about. First of all I asked 'im if 'e thought I was me brother, because I wasn't in that line. 'E said no, 'e knew me brother and it wasn't in 'is line. So naturally I said: "Wot's in it for me?" and 'e said "Fifty nicker." So naturally I said: "When do I get it?" and 'e said "When you've done it." So naturally I said: "When I've done wot?" And then 'e told me.'

Mr Adams relapsed into silence.

'What did the man tell you?'

'I told yer.'

'No you didn't. You just said he'd pay you fifty pounds when you'd done it.'

'That's right. I told yer. That's what 'e said.'

'But what did he tell you you were to do for the fifty pounds?'

' 'E said it was dead easy. There wasn't nothing to it, 'e said. So naturally I said "if there ain't nothing to it, why do I get fifty nicker?" So 'e said: " 'Cos that's the price; ain't it enough?" So I said: "All right. Wot is it?" And then 'e told me.'

'But what did he tell you?'

'Wot I 'ad ter do.'

'But what was that?'

'Wot I did.'

'You mean he told you to go and sit in the park and that a man would come along and drop a glove and throw a newspaper into a litter basket, and that you were to go and take them to the police?'

'That's right,' said Jo. 'Put the words into his mouth. Is he telling the story, or are you?'

'Is that what happened, Mr Adams?' persisted the judge.

'Near enough,' said Adams.

'And did you get your fifty pounds?'

'Oh, yes, 'e played fair all right. 'Arf on the day and 'arf later. Oh, yes, 'e paid all right. Still don't know why 'e paid as much. But naturally yer can't turn down fifty nicker, can yer? 'E was quite right. It was dead easy.'

'Who was this man who paid you £50?'

'I dunno. 'Adn't seen 'im afore.'

'How did he get hold of you?'

'I dunno. 'E just came. Expect 'e 'eard that I did odd jobs for people.'

'This was about the oddest, I expect,' said the judge.

'I wouldn't say that,' said Adams, 'but it was paid the best.'

'Well, Mr Hampton,' said the judge, 'I don't know whether you heard any of that, but may I ask how much you got for sitting in the park and telling about it afterwards? All right, you needn't answer,' he went on hurriedly, as he saw that Miles was changing colour again.

'Now, Mrs Barnwell,' said the judge, 'are you still prepared to deny that, apart from the evidence of the man who was present when your husband was killed and the police evidence, you procured the whole of this evidence against Mr Walsh?'

'Of course I am,' said Jo. 'You can't bully or cajole me, as you have these other witnesses. I've never seen such a disgraceful performance. Witnesses fainting all over the place, evidence given at the pistol point, the police turned away, and then you have the impertinence to ask me if I deny having concocted a case which has been believed by a jury, believed by the Court of Criminal Appeal and believed by the Home Secretary. My case is the only true one, but your methods would twist any case, however true. You can do what you like about it, but so shall I. The newspapers and Members of Parliament and the Lord Chancellor will be told all about this. And there are too many witnesses here for you to deny it. You're almost worse than he is,' and she pointed to Lonsdale. 'After all, he has got himself to look after. You can't so much blame a man for doing that. But you—you're so puffed up with your pride in being a judge that you love to interfere in other people's affairs, which are nothing whatever to do with you. The case has been decided. It's over. There was only one thing for you to do—hand this man and his confederates over to the police as soon as possible.'

'Mr Walsh,' said the judge, 'I shall have to consider most carefully what I am to do about this, but it is right to tell you now that, in spite of the unorthodox, unofficial manner in which this enquiry has come before me . . .'

'Unorthodox!' sneered Jo, interrupting.

'Unlawful, if you prefer it,' went on the judge. 'In spite of all that, I am quite satisfied that there was a gross mis-carriage of justice at your trial. I am quite satisfied that the whole of the main evidence against you was fabricated by or at the instigation of this woman. I am quite satisfied that, had the true facts been known to the jury, they would unhesitatingly have acquitted you. I shall write to the Home Secretary to that effect, and give him my detailed reasons for my opinion. Unfortunately, as far as I can see, no proceedings whatever can be taken against Mrs Barnwell or any of her witnesses. They were brought here by force or by a trick, and their evidence has unquestionably been procured by threats and duress. What is to happen to you and your confederates for the methods you have seen fit to adopt, it is not for me to say. But, criminal though those methods have been, you are at any rate entitled to say that, as far as I can see, unless you had adopted them, your innocence could not have been made known. In these circumstances it may be that the Home Secretary will be able to take a different view of your behaviour and of that of your colleagues than seemed possible a day or two ago. But I must make it plain that that does not lie in my hands and that all I can do is to make the report which I have just indicated. I now call upon you to keep your promise to allow the police to be summoned and to give yourself up to them.'

'Certainly,' said Lonsdale, 'but, first of all, I am going to give those who have assisted me an opportunity of getting well out of the way. I see no reason why they should take any unnecessary risks, whatever view the authorities may eventually take. Spikey, tell everyone who wants to be off to go as quickly as possible. Anyone who wishes may remain. I suggest we wait a quarter of an hour before summoning the police. Perhaps Spikey would produce some drinks for those who would like to wait. Forgive me for continuing to act as host for the moment, Sir George. I will hand over to you as soon as my assistants have left. And I should make it plain that we have brought our drinks with us.'

'I take it I may leave now?' said Jo.

'Certainly, Jo,' said Lonsdale.

'Just a word in your private ear before I go,' said Jo.

She took Lonsdale aside and whispered:

'Don't think you'll get away with this. I'll get you yet.'

'Perhaps we shall get each other,' said Lonsdale.

'I loathe you,' said Jo.

'You don't,' said Lonsdale and, much to the judge's surprise, he kissed her good-bye.

'You wait,' said Jo, and went hurriedly out of the room.

'All right boys, beat it,' said Spikey. 'I'll 'op it after the drinks.'

Within ten minutes no one was left in the judge's house except the judge and his staff, Lonsdale and Angela, Charles, Mr and Mrs Broadwater, Mrs Meadowes, Miles, Adams and Allwinter.

'I'm most grateful to you, Sir George,' said Lonsdale, 'for the trouble you have taken over this matter, and I do apologise for any inconvenience you and your staff have been caused. I would also like to thank Mr Southdown and Mr Broadwater for their help and to apologise to them and Mrs Broadwater. I should include in my apologies Mr Allwinter, against whom I have no complaint.'

'Well,' said the judge, 'I don't think we'd better discuss the matter any further. It will obviously be the subject of a further enquiry by the Home Office. It will certainly give the newspapers something to talk about.'

In a corner of the room Broadwater chatted to his wife.

'What a bit of luck I insisted on coming,' she said. 'This is better than anything I could have hoped for. Think of the publicity.'

'My dear Mary,' said her husband, 'you're entirely wrong. Certainly I shall have something for my reminiscences but, if you think that the publicity in this case is going to advance me one foot nearer to the Bench, you're very much mistaken. Judges are not appointed by the number of times they appear in the paper or the number of cocktail parties they attend. In the old days undoubtedly politics had something to do with it, but fortunately today they hardly enter into it. I'm not saying there aren't some bad appointments sometimes. There are. And that gives me a chance.'

'Don't be modest, darling,' said Mary, 'you'd be a very good appointment.'

'That's a thing which no one can say. That's why there are bad appointments. You get a man who's first-class at the Bar but makes a rotten judge. And you get a man who isn't much of an advocate and only has a moderate practice who'd make a first-class judge, if only they knew it. On the whole, of course, you can get a fair idea of whether a man is likely to be a reasonably good judge. In most cases you might say it's a pretty safe bet. But there are always the exceptions. Surprise appointments which turn out well and expected appointments which turn out badly.'

'I don't mind which you are, darling,' said Mary, 'so long as you're appointed.'

Angela was in the meantime chatting to Charles.

'I think you were wonderful,' she said. 'No, I really mean it. Mark you, I take great credit to myself for having picked you out. You fitted into the scheme of things so well. I'd no notion why father wanted a barrister, but I can see now all right why he insisted on the qualifications he mentioned. How right he was. And how right I was both in my judge and my counsel.'

'I'd like to think I was your counsel,' said Charles.

'Would you really?' said Angela. 'You don't know me very well. And my father's in gaol, or will be very soon.'

'You don't know me very well,' said Charles, 'but I can put that right, if you'll let me.'

'You can start right now.'

'Will you dine with me this evening?'

'I'd love it. It's such a shame I shan't be able to dine with daddy. But it won't be long now.'

'I think I ought to warn you,' said Charles, 'that it may take a little longer than you think.'

Angela became anxious.

'You're not suggesting . . .' she began.

'Oh, no,' said Charles. 'I'm sure they'll give him a free pardon. But a thing like this must take time. They don't just have a drawer with free pardons in it, and take one out. Don't forget, the Home Office knows nothing of all this, and though, with the weight of Halliday's authority, I'm quite sure everything will be all right, they've got to enquire into the matter. And that must take some time.'

'What do you mean by "some time"? How long?'

'Well, of course, I can't say with any certainty. But days at the least. Possibly weeks. I don't think more. But suppose the Home Secretary orders an enquiry. First of all he's got to appoint someone to preside at it. Then they've got to arrange about the place where to hold it, the witnesses who are to be summoned, counsel who are to be briefed. You can't rush important things like this. After all, your father has been convicted and his appeal dismissed. You can't scrub that out in a couple of minutes. Indeed, it's very fortunate for you that you've got someone like Halliday on your side. If it were one or two of the other judges I know, well, first of all, you might never have got to this stage; and secondly, even if you had, there would be less alacrity on the part of the Home Office to jump to it. No, you couldn't have had a better choice than Halliday.'

'You really chose him for me, but I chose you. I can take full credit for that.'

Mrs Meadowes, Miles and Adams had a little conversation with each other.

'Wot's it all about?' said Adams.

'Blessed if I know,' said Mrs Meadowes. 'When do we

go 'ome? And 'ow do we get there? I'd come 'ere to win a football pool. Shan't go in for them any more, if this is wot 'appens. I don't know what my Ernie will say. 'E ain't all that partial to judges.'

'Personally,' said Miles, 'I wish I'd never had anything to do with it.'

'We'll get our names in the papers,' said Adams. 'And our pictures, I shouldn't wonder.'

'Yes,' said Miles, suddenly remembering his B.B.C. interviews, and brightening a little at the thought. 'Yes, there is that. Look,' he added suddenly, 'the three of us might give an interview on T.V.'

Miles had originally thought of having a solo appearance but it occurred to him that the contrast between him and Mrs Meadowes and Adams might show him up to advantage.

'What d'you say?' he asked. 'You leave it to me, and I'll try and fix it up. We ought to get £10 apiece for it. What about it?'

'I don't mind,' said Mrs Meadowes, 'so long as they don't ask me a lot of silly questions.'

'I'm afraid that's inevitable,' said Miles. 'It's a very difficult job, you know, interviewing someone. People think it's dead easy. But it isn't, not by a long way. Suppose you were interviewing me now, how would you begin?'

'Well, I know that one,' said Adams. 'I seen it. I'd say "Good evening, Mr whatever your name is." That's right, isn't it?'

'Yes,' said Miles, 'that's all right so far, but how d'you go on after that?'

'I know that too,' said Adams. 'So good of you to come tonight.'

'Jolly good,' said Miles. 'And after that?'

'Now you've got me,' said Adams. 'But then it ain't my job. But I didn't do so bad, did I?'

'It was just like the real thing,' said Mrs Meadowes. 'We got a new one coming when we're married. Ernie says 'e can't abide those small screens. Can't see enough of the girls.'

'My brother made ours,' said Adams.

'He's a T.V. expert, is he?' asked Miles.

' 'E knows where to find 'em,' said Adams.

At this point the judge went to the telephone.

'Well, Mr Walsh,' he said, 'I think time's up. Your chaps have had ample time to get away now.'

'It's very good of you to have waited,' said Lonsdale. 'Which reminds me that I've never thanked you for sending the police away.'

'Well,' said the judge, 'I can't pretend I'm very happy about having done that. But it seemed to me that, if I didn't get to the bottom of things there and then, no one might ever do so. I took a chance. I hope I was right.'

'I'm sure you were,' said Lonsdale. 'But then, of course, I suppose I'm prejudiced.'

'Hullo,' said the judge on the telephone, 'can I speak to the inspector, please? This is Sir George Halliday speaking.'

'Hold the line, please, sir,' said the sergeant. 'Can you beat it,' he said to the inspector, 'it's the old boy on the telephone. I wonder what he wants.'

The inspector went to the telephone.

'Inspector,' said the judge, 'I have an escaped prisoner here. His name is Lonsdale Walsh.'

'Lonsdale Walsh!' said the inspector incredulously.

'That's right, inspector. Will you send for him at once? I don't think he'll run away, but come at once, please.'

'I *can* beat it,' said the inspector to the sergeant. 'He's got Walsh up there with him. If you ask me, he's had him there all the time. Now why on earth should he do that?'

'I'd be a superintendent if I knew,' said the sergeant.

CHAPTER SEVENTEEN

Public Enquiry

THE same day Lonsdale was taken back to prison. He was almost immediately taken before the governor. The judge had given Lonsdale a letter addressed to the governor, who had read it before the interview.

'This is all very well,' said the governor, 'but you can't do this sort of thing. This letter says that in Mr Justice Halliday's view you were wrongly convicted. Well, I'm not a judge. I'm just a prison governor. There's no doubt you were lawfully committed to my prison and unlawfully broke out. As far as I'm concerned, everyone here is guilty.'

'I quite understand, sir,' said Lonsdale, 'but what else could I do? I had tried all the lawful channels, the Courts and the Home Secretary and my Member of Parliament. If you remember, I came before you, sir, and asked what I could do. You told me to wait ten years.'

'So you should have,' said the governor. 'It's unlawful to break out of prison.'

'It was a choice of evils, sir,' said Lonsdale. 'I had to break the law in order to have my conviction set aside. If I'd done nothing, no one else would. I should have rotted here.'

'Rules were made to be kept,' said the governor. 'There are a lot of people here who say they're innocent, but, if we let them all out to try to prove it, we'd have no one left in the end. They'd all say they wanted to prove their innocence.'

'Mine is rather an exceptional case, sir,' said Lonsdale.

'Exactly,' said the governor. 'Hard cases make bad law. You can't provide for every exceptional case. You've put everyone to an enormous amount of trouble and expense. D'you know that I personally have interviewed nearly every man in the prison to see if I could find out where you were going?'

'I'm extremely sorry, sir,' said Lonsdale, 'but, if you'll put yourself in my position, what else was there to do?'

'I refuse to put myself in your position.'

'At least I gave myself up when I was satisfied that something would be done about my case.'

'Most considerate of you,' said the governor. 'D'you realise how much you've cost the country up till now? I'm a humane man, I hope. But I won't stand for lawlessness. How did you get out anyway?'

'I climbed over the wall.'

'Oh, you did, did you? That was an outrageous thing to do.'

'I couldn't very well walk out of the gate, sir.'

'Don't be impertinent. You had outside help, I suppose.'

'Oh, yes,' said Lonsdale. 'They threw a rope ladder over to me.'

'Then you needed some inside help as well.'

'Only one,' said Lonsdale.

'I imagine you're not going to tell me who he was.'

'No, sir.'

'Well, I don't grumble at that, but it'd be better for you if you did. You've committed a number of offences now, whatever the truth about the original charge. And you can be punished for them.'

'I must take a chance on that, sir.'

'Very well,' said the governor. 'I shan't deal with you myself. I shall wait for the visiting justices, but I should make it plain that personally I'm against you. What's the good of a prison if people can escape from it because they

F

want to prove they're innocent? It's ridiculous. Take him away.'

The first announcement of Lonsdale's recapture was given some prominence in the newspapers, but there was no hint in the first news of the sensation which was to follow. At first there were only rumours, and passages began to appear such as:

'It is said that there will be surprising developments when the facts surrounding Walsh's escape are made public. It has been suggested that for a time he hid in a High Court judge's house.'

Eventually there were so many semi-accurate and inaccurate statements made that the Home Office issued an official pronouncement. But even this was in somewhat guarded language.

'Lonsdale Walsh, who recently escaped from prison and was subsequently recaptured, during his period of freedom gave certain information to Mr Justice Halliday, as a result of which a report from the judge is now being considered by the Home Secretary. Certain other persons also gave information to Mr Justice Halliday.'

A crop of rumours then began to circulate as to the nature of the information given to the judge and the names of the people, in addition to Lonsdale, who gave that information. Finally, Miles went to one of the television authorities and offered to tell his story at an interview. The persons responsible for authorising such an interview immediately communicated with the Home Office and asked if there was any objection to this story being published, to which the reply was received that the Home Secretary would much prefer that nothing was said in public pending a further official statement, which was being issued. The note added that the responsibility for any inaccuracies or mis-statements would be that of the television authorities. 'It is also possible,' added the note, 'that questions of contempt of Court might be involved.'

So Miles had to wait. But his visit certainly speeded up things.

Three days later the Home Office announced that the Home Secretary was proposing to appoint three Supreme Court judges to enquire into the circumstances surrounding the escape and recapture of Lonsdale Walsh, including any matters which might throw light on the question whether there was a miscarriage of justice at his trial for murder.

Soon after, Lord Justice Manners, Mr Justice Swann and Mr Justice Tennant were appointed, and the public waited with interest to hear and read what would transpire.

The result was beyond their wildest expectations, because one of the chief witnesses at the enquiry was Mr Justice Halliday himself. The whole of the circumstances of the house imprisonment of the judge and the kidnapping or enticing of the witnesses was made known. There were two main questions to be answered. The first was whether Lonsdale had been wrongly convicted and, if the answer to the first question was Yes, the second question was what was to be done about the methods adopted by him to prove his innocence.

The tribunal decided to go into the first question first.

'It is true,' said Lord Justice Manners, 'that in point of time the escape and kidnapping came first, but the unanimous view of the Tribunal is this. If we are not satisfied that there was any miscarriage of justice, then there is no real point in our enquiring into the other matters. The law must take its course and those responsible for breaking it, including, of course, the escaped prisoner, should be proceeded against for such crimes as they have committed. If, however, we are satisfied that Walsh's conviction for murder was procured by perjured evidence and ought not to stand, we must then proceed to consider what, in our view, in the public interest ought to be done about these other offences.'

Lonsdale was represented at the enquiry by Charles, while the Attorney-General appeared for the Crown with a Treasury junior. All the other people concerned were represented by counsel. In opening the case the Attorney-General said:

'Although this is not a rehearing of the case tried at the Central Criminal Court, I have considered it desirable, subject to the view of the Tribunal, to have present all the available witnesses who gave evidence there, and, of course, everyone available who was in Mr Justice Halliday's house. One thing I should make plain. It is the view of the Crown that nothing said in Mr Justice Halliday's house could be used in evidence against the person who said it, at any subsequent criminal proceedings against that person. They were detained by force in that house and undoubtedly that threat of force to some extent at least compelled them to make their statements. On the other hand, anything said now by any witness can, of course, be used in evidence for or against that witness in any subsequent proceedings. Accordingly, the Tribunal may wish to warn some of the witnesses that they are not bound to answer any questions which might incriminate them. Unless, of course, the Tribunal take the view that they should be compelled to answer such questions. In that case, of course, the answers would not later be available against them.'

Lord Justice Manners, after consultation with his colleagues, then announced that they were proposing to treat the proceedings for that purpose as a court of law and that no witnesses would be compelled to incriminate themselves.

The first witness to be called was Mr Allwinter. He gave similar evidence to that which he gave to Mr Justice Halliday and Charles was then asked if he wished to cross-examine. Before doing so he thanked the Tribunal for allowing him to appear at all.

'As I am a witness to what took place before Mr Justice Halliday, I should, of course, normally have refused this brief. Indeed, I should automatically have refused it had your Lordships not indicated that, in view of my client's very strong desire to have my services on this occasion, it would be proper in the exceptional circumstances for me to appear.'

He then proceeded to cross-examine Mr Allwinter.

'Mr Allwinter,' he began, 'a lot of water has flowed under the bridge since I last questioned you, has it not?'

'It has indeed.'

'And you yourself saw it first trickle and then burst into flood.'

'If you like to put it that way, yes.'

'Now, Mr Allwinter, all you actually saw of this occurrence was a vague impression of a car moving and then a man left dead after having been struck by it, and the car moving off swiftly afterwards?'

'Something like that.'

'When I questioned you last time, you were obviously of the opinion that it was a case of murder.'

'I was.'

'And when I pointed out the possibility of it being a hit-and-run driver, you referred to the "other evidence".'

'That is correct.'

'By the "other evidence" you meant the witnesses who made statements to Mr Justice Halliday, and the man Meadowes who died?'

'Yes.'

'You have now had the advantage of seeing their performances before Mr Justice Halliday?'

'Yes.'

'They were rather different from their performances at the Old Bailey, were they not?'

'They were indeed.'

'Are you still of the opinion that this was a case of

murder or was it not just as likely, or indeed much more likely, the case of a hit-and-run driver?'

'I feel quite sure now that it was a hit-and-run driver.'

'Thank you,' said Charles, and sat down.

'But I gather,' said Lord Justice Manners, 'that previously you were convinced that it was a case of murder.'

'That is so.'

'That was because you had heard other evidence?'

'Yes.'

'And now you are convinced that it was a case of a hit-and-run driver?'

'Yes.'

'So the truth of the matter is surely this, Mr Allwinter. As far as your own eyes and ears at the time of the occurrence are concerned, you haven't the faintest idea whether it was murder, manslaughter or no offence at all by the driver, except that he or she failed to stop?'

'I suppose that's right, my Lord,' said Mr Allwinter.

'That shows the danger of paying attention to other people's statements when you are supposed to be saying only what you saw and heard yourself.'

'It is only fair to Mr Allwinter,' said Charles, 'to mention that he didn't in the first instance say anything except what he had seen and heard. It was only when I questioned him that he showed what his views were.'

'In other words you say, Mr Southdown, that, as far as his actual evidence about the occurrence is concerned, Mr Allwinter did not allow it to become coloured by his opinion.'

'That is quite correct, my Lord.'

'Then I should congratulate Mr Allwinter,' said Lord Justice Manners, 'rather than criticise him. In most accident cases witnesses who have formed a view as to the cause, allow their evidence to become violently coloured by their views. Such evidence is pretty well valueless.'

'Please don't think I intend to be offensive to Mr All-

winter,' said Mr Justice Swann, 'but his evidence, dis-
passionately given as it is, is also pretty well valueless. We
all know that the unfortunate man was killed by a car.
And that is all he can tell us. Presumably his injuries and
position in the road were such that this could have been
deduced quite simply by his body being found in the road.
That the car did not stop was plain because it was not
waiting by the body.'

'It might have been a horse and cart,' put in Mr Justice
Tennant.

'Or an omnibus,' said Lord Justice Manners.

'Or a motor cycle,' continued Mr Justice Tennant.

'Or van,' said Lord Justice Manners. 'We have to thank
Mr Allwinter for telling us that it was a car.'

'Does it help us much to know that it was a car?' asked
Mr Justice Swann. 'What we want to know is whether the
person in charge of the vehicle ran the man over deliberately or by accident. As far as Mr Allwinter's evidence is
concerned, the man might just have been found dead.'

'Surely,' said Lord Justice Manners, 'what we want to
know is whether the vehicle, whatever it was, was driven
by Meadowes. If it wasn't, that's an end of the first
question we are invited to consider. Meadowes himself
cannot tell us, and we have to find out from all the other
evidence whether he was driving. Mr Allwinter, admirable
witness though he is, doesn't help us in the least about
that.'

Mr Justice Swann leaned back in his chair with an air
of finality. His point had been established.

'Perhaps then, Mr Allwinter can be allowed to go home,'
suggested Lord Justice Manners. 'Does anyone in the
case want him to remain? Do you, Mr Attorney?'

'No, thank you, my Lord,' said the Attorney-General.

'Does counsel for any other party wish him to stay?'

One by one, counsel got up and said that his client did
not require any further evidence from Mr Allwinter.

'Very well,' said Lord Justice Manners. 'Thank you, Mr Allwinter. We shall not want you any more. You may go away.'

'Do I have to?' asked Mr Allwinter. 'I'd like to hear what happens.'

The next three witnesses were very simply disposed of. They were Miles, Adams and Mrs Meadowes. One by one their respective counsel got up and said they had taken the responsibility of advising their clients not to give evidence. That is to say, they would, of course, go through the formality of going into the witness box and being sworn but, when it came to answering any material questions, they would claim privilege on the grounds that the answers might incriminate them.

'You talk of the formality of being sworn,' said Mr Justice Swann. 'From what you are saying, it suggests that your clients considered it a very unimportant formality.'

'If your Lordship pleases,' said counsel for one of those witnesses.

'I don't please at all,' said Mr Justice Swann. 'Your clients, having given vital evidence upon which a man was convicted of murder, now, if you please, haven't the courage to try to put right any wrong they may have done by their original evidence.'

'I don't please at all either, if I may say so,' said counsel, 'but, in all the circumstances, I think it the proper course for my client to take, and my learned colleagues take the same view.'

'This is tantamount to an admission that their original evidence was false,' said Lord Justice Manners.

'I cannot make any admissions,' said counsel.

'We are not asking you to do so,' said Lord Justice Manners. 'But, before we can relieve your clients of the obligation of answering the material questions, we have to be satisfied that, to force them to answer, might reasonably result in their incriminating themselves. You have not merely to admit that, but to assert it.'

'We all assert it, my Lord.'

'Very well, then. The only way in which your clients could incriminate themselves is by admitting that they had committed perjury at the original trial.'

'That is not the only way, my Lord,' said counsel. 'They might have to admit other offences as well.'

'You mean such offences as conspiring to defeat the ends of justice?'

'That is so, my Lord.'

'And you all claim privilege for your clients on the grounds that, if we compelled them to answer, they might render themselves liable to be indicted not only for perjury but for another offence or offences as well?'

'That is so, my Lord.'

'And you each make this claim of privilege on behalf of your clients, bearing in mind your responsibility to the Court as counsel and after careful consultation with your respective clients?'

'Yes, my Lord.'

'Very well, then,' said Lord Justice Manners. 'I repeat that this is tantamount to an admission by these witnesses that they endeavoured successfully to swear away a man's liberty by perjured evidence.'

'I am not in a position to say anything as to that,' said counsel.

The three judges conferred for a few moments. Then Lord Justice Manners said:

'We know that we can completely trust counsel neither to mislead the Court nor to make a dubious claim for privilege of this kind without disclosing the circumstances giving rise to the doubt. All three counsel have made it quite plain that, if their clients were compelled to answer the questions material to this enquiry, they might well find themselves prosecuted criminally. No one is required to

give evidence himself in this way and we accordingly
allow the claim of privilege in reliance on counsel's statements and, of course, on what we know of the case. But
the witnesses will remain within the precincts of this
building until the enquiry has been completed.'

The next witness was Jo.

'I gather from your silence,' said Lord Justice Manners
to Jo's counsel, 'that your client does not wish to claim
privilege.'

'She does not, my Lord.'

Jo then went into the witness box and gave much the
same evidence as she gave at the trial. She stoutly denied
that she had procured any of the witnesses and she
repeated her explanations, such as they were, for not
producing the photograph earlier and for her sudden
exclamation before Mr Justice Halliday. In view of the
refusal of the other witnesses to give evidence, hers was an
impossible task and she knew it. But at least she stuck to
her guns and made no admissions of any kind. When her
evidence had been completed, Lonsdale went into the
witness box.

He gave his evidence well and frankly and appeared
obviously to be telling the truth. When he had finished,
the judges consulted for a few minutes and then Lord
Justice Manners said:

'We have without difficulty come to a clear conclusion
on the first question we have been asked to consider. We
will put our reasons into writing, but it is right to say at
once that we are all firmly convinced that there was a
gross miscarriage of justice when Mr Walsh was convicted.
We must now, therefore, consider the second far more
difficult question, which really comes to this. To what
extent are a man and his collaborators free from criminal
responsibility when they break the law in order to remedy
an injustice? It is an extremely difficult problem. And
perhaps I was wrong to put it so generally. For example,

it is plain that if a man charged with capital murder is acquitted and subsequently confesses to the crime, it would plainly be murder for someone to kill him, even though he ought to have been executed. I think I must revise what I said. We have to consider whether the steps taken in this case were morally justified and whether, although amounting to crimes, they ought or ought not to be visited with the normal consequences of committing a crime.'

'There is, my Lords, a further question which I am instructed to raise,' said counsel for Jo. 'I do so with some embarrassment, but I am quite sure that it is my duty to refer to it, in view of my instructions.'

'What is the point?' asked Lord Justice Manners.

'It is the conduct of Mr Justice Halliday,' said counsel. 'With the greatest possible respect to the learned judge, he appears to have rendered himself liable, certainly to a civil action. Whether or not his actions amounted to a crime I leave it to your Lordships to say.'

'What on earth are you talking about?' said Lord Justice Manners, with some heat. 'The learned judge was in effect kidnapped, like your client, and forced to act as he did. He appears to have acted in a most courageous and balanced manner in very difficult circumstances.'

'My Lord,' said counsel, 'I don't dispute that for a moment. And up to a certain stage in the matter the learned judge was completely blameless.'

'When then do you say he incurred some kind of liability for his actions?'

'My Lord, when he deliberately sent away the police.'

'When he sent away the police? What are you talking about?' said Lord Justice Manners.

'My Lords, you have not yet heard the evidence, but the learned judge will himself tell you, I am quite sure, that at a fairly late stage in the proceedings, if I may so

term them, the police arrived at the house and he sent
them away again.'

'To prevent a pitched battle, no doubt,' said Lord
Justice Manners.

'No, my Lord. It is perfectly true that only two police
officers arrived and that they would have been heavily
outnumbered and outgunned, but the learned judge did
not send them away to get reinforcements, he sent them
away so that he could proceed with the enquiry he had
been forced to start. And the police will tell you, my
Lords, that he gave them the impression that nothing
was wrong but that he was busy.'

'Is that correct, Mr Attorney?' asked Lord Justice
Manners.

'Substantially, yes, my Lord,' said the Attorney-
General.

'Well,' said Lord Justice Manners, 'you have brought
the matter to our attention and no doubt it falls within
the scope of our enquiry. We had better wait until we
hear exactly what happened.'

The Attorney-General then called Mr Justice Halliday
to give his account of what happened. When he had
finished, Lord Justice Manners conferred with his
colleagues.

'We are a little troubled, Sir George,' he said, after a
short consultation, 'about this matter of the police being
sent away. As we understand the position, until that
moment you were all held prisoner in your house?'

'That is so, my Lords.'

'But then you were permitted to interview the police
inspector and sergeant and you could have asked them to
bring help to release you. Is that right?'

'That is quite correct, my Lords.'

'In fact, however, you did nothing of the kind but put
off the police as though nothing were the matter and went
back to continue your enquiry.'

'Quite true, my Lords.'

'Well, Sir George, whatever the motives or reasons which prompted you to act in this way, didn't your behaviour identify yourself, to some extent at any rate, with your captors as far as the other captives were concerned? For example, Mrs Barnwell wished to leave the house but was prevented from doing so by the threat of force. If you had asked the police to bring up reinforcements, that would not have happened. May it not, therefore, be said that by your deliberate abstention from seeking help, when help could have been obtained, you became party to the false imprisonment of Mrs Barnwell?'

'My Lords,' said Mr Justice Halliday, 'while I am making no formal admission on the subject, I recognise that, as a pure proposition of law, that may be right. I had a very difficult choice to make. Shall I tell your Lordships why I acted as I did?'

'If you please, Sir George.'

'At the precise moment when the police arrived I had reached a critical stage in the enquiry I had been compelled to make. Your Lordships have now held that there was a gross miscarriage of justice at Mr Walsh's trial. At the time the police arrived I had come to the conclusion that that might have been the case, but I also realised that, unless I could pursue the enquiry at once, it might well be that it could never be satisfactorily concluded. It was a case of striking while the iron was hot. Three witnesses have before your Lordships refused to give evidence on the ground that they might incriminate themselves. Had the enquiry come to an end at the time the police arrived, it is at the very least possible and, in my view, probable, that those witnesses would have sufficiently recovered themselves and received sufficient advice and encouragement from other sources to prompt them to continue the conspiracy to defeat the ends of justice, which your Lordships have held they have impliedly admitted. Of course, my view may have been wrong, but I do not think it was. The position was, therefore, in my opinion, that, if I called for help from the police, it might never have been possible to establish the innocence of this man, and he would have had to complete his sentence of life imprisonment. The view which I held then, and which I respectfully adhere to, was that in such circumstances the sanctity of human liberty for such a length of time was more important than the comparatively short time for which our imprisonment would continue. If by my conduct I have rendered myself liable in damages to Mrs Barnwell or anyone else, if anything more than a nominal sum should in the circumstances be paid to them, I consider the money well spent. But I hasten to add that I think the Treasury ought to pay it. As far as crime is concerned, I entirely dispute that my action in failing to ask for police help amounted to any crime known to the English law. If it did, the law ought to be altered.'

'No doubt, Sir George,' said Lord Justice Manners, with the suspicion of a smile, 'the Attorney-General will address us on the law if necessary. Thank you for your explanation. Does anyone want to ask Sir George any questions?'

Jo's counsel got up. 'Sir George,' he said, 'you agree that Mrs Barnwell wished to leave the house and was prevented from doing so?'

'I have already said so.'

'Did she not protest in the strongest possible terms about your conduct in sending the police away?'

'She did so, as you have said, in the strongest possible terms.'

'So that, in effect, you deliberately kept her in the house against her will.'

'I did not actually keep her, but I put it out of her and my power to get released.'

'Presumably you realised that you were doing this—

that you were unnecessarily prolonging Mrs Barnwell's and your own imprisonment?'

'I did not consider that aspect of the matter at the time, I confess, but I agree that it was implicit in what I did. Perhaps I ought to add that it is possible that by my action I saved injury or life. I should make it plain that that was not the object of my sending the police away. I believed that, as soon as the enquiry was over, Mr Walsh would keep his word, send his men away and surrender to the police. But I also believed that he and his assistants were quite determined that the enquiry should be completed before his recapture. It is at least possible, therefore, that, had I called for help, there would have been a pitched battle between the police and our captors. I repeat that I had not that in mind. But your client may care to consider that it is possible that I saved her from injury or even death. Nor was she kept a prisoner for a moment longer than was necessary to complete the enquiry. I cannot conceive that the same thing will ever happen again, but, if it did, I think I should feel obliged to act in the same way.'

The judge completed his evidence and then Lonsdale gave evidence about his escape and the reasons for it. He refused to divulge the names of his associates and was not pressed to do so. Again he gave his account well and with obvious sincerity.

'The governor of my prison suggested that I ought to have waited in prison until I was released,' he said. 'I quite understand his point of view. No governor can view escapes with equanimity or, if I may say so, without bias. It was his job to keep me inside. It was my job to get outside. Had there been any legal method of achieving my object, I should, of course, have pursued it, but I had exhausted all legal methods. What else was there for me to do?'

That indeed was an unanswerable question. In order

to have his case reviewed, he had not only to escape but to take the other illegal and dangerous steps which he had taken. When Lonsdale had finished his evidence, Charles took up the burden on his behalf.

'Your Lordships have now proclaimed my client to have been the subject of a disgraceful conspiracy and to have been wrongfully convicted. We know that occasionally such cases may occur, but this one has only come to light by reason of my client's illegal activities. It would, in my respectful submission, be an outrage if he were now prosecuted for the crimes he was forced to commit. I agree that there is less to be said for his accomplices who took on the job as one of business and for which they have been well paid. But my client has particularly asked that your Lordships should hold that no proceedings ought to be taken against any of them who can be found or identified. For certain it is that without their help my client would never have been able to do what he did. Their moral guilt may be rather more than my client's but, even in their case, they knew they were assisting in an attempt to prove my client's innocence. Whether or not they believed in it I do not know, but they may well have been impressed by the amount my client was prepared to spend on the undertaking.'

'Mr Southdown,' said Lord Justice Manners, 'I gather that most of your client's accomplices could not be identified, as they were masked.'

'That is so, my Lord.'

'Speaking for myself only, I must say that I should at least think it rather bad luck on anyone who was not so disguised being charged, while his associates get off scot free.'

'The same remark could apply to any burglary,' said Mr Justice Swann.

'Of course it could,' said Lord Justice Manners, 'but this is very different from a burglary. Indeed, the main

object was not a felonious one at all. It wasn't a crime at
all. The object was to procure an enquiry. That is all. The
methods used to procure it were, of course, criminal, but
no one was injured or more than inconvenienced as a
result, and, as the object was a good one, I should have
thought that the pursuit of the perpetrators would not be
particularly desirable. Although public feeling is by no
means always the right guide in these matters, there is no
doubt whatever but that the public would be very much
against the prosecution of any such proceedings. The only
proceedings which, in my personal view, ought to be
taken are proceedings against those who successfully
sought the conviction of Mr Walsh by a criminal conspiracy. But there is obviously in law insufficient evidence
to bring them to trial, however loudly the facts speak for
themselves.'

Eventually the Tribunal completed its hearing and, in
due course, its findings were published. They completely
vindicated Lonsdale and recommended that no proceedings should be taken against anyone. Lonsdale had been
released immediately after the public hearing. He received
many letters of congratulation, including one from Jo.

'You've done very well,' she wrote, 'and I congratulate
you. But don't think I'm going to let it rest at this. Love,
Jo.'

Lonsdale smiled, and threw the note into the fire.

A little later on he had a visit from the Boss. He had
asked him to call.

'How nice to see you again,' he said, after the Boss had
been shown in. 'I do want to tell you how grateful I am
for all you did.'

'Not at all,' said the Boss. 'It was a real pleasure and
paid for handsomely. I wish all my customers were as
forthcoming. D'you know, I've almost felt like retiring.
But I should get bored, you know. I shall take a holiday,
of course.'

'Why don't you write a book?' suggested Lonsdale. 'That's quite a recognised profession for retired crim . . . retired people to take up. I expect you could tell a few interesting stories. Change the names, of course, and alter them about.'

'I'm not much good with a pen,' said the Boss. 'I wasn't at school. My essays were dreadful. Always getting into trouble over them.'

'Oh, well,' said Lonsdale, 'it was only a passing thought. I'd hate to see anyone, who's been as useful to me as you, languishing in prison. I gather that they do catch up with you sometimes.'

'It has been known,' said the Boss. 'It's my own fault really. But I like to see a job's done really well, and that does mean paying visits to the site from time to time. But, after all, I shouldn't have got my practice together if I hadn't done that. So I can't really complain.'

'But you'll have to retire some time,' said Lonsdale. 'Why not make it now? You're still young enough to enjoy life.'

'That's the trouble. When I'm older I may not want the excitement I need now. You've no idea how thrilling it is to watch a well-prepared plan carried out. I got a terrific kick out of arranging yours. No mountaineer retires until he's past it. He just can't give it up. It'll be the same with me. However, let's hope I'm lucky. They haven't had me for some time.'

'They'll be on the look-out for you now,' said Lonsdale. 'I expect they know you were behind this.'

'I'm sure they do,' said the Boss. 'They know that no one else could have done it so well.'

CHAPTER EIGHTEEN

Counsel's Opinion

Two days after Lonsdale's release from prison, Jo walked into a solicitor's office. She had an appointment to see Mr Manage of Streak & Manage. As soon as she had sat down she came to the point.

'Mr Manage,' she said, 'would your firm have any objection to bringing an action against a High Court judge for conspiracy?'

Mr Manage brightened perceptibly.

'Mrs Barnwell,' he said, 'subject only to considerations of professional propriety, my firm would be delighted to bring an action against a High Court judge for conspiracy, bottomry, barratry or even for plain straightforward negligence. I personally should welcome the opportunity. Shall I tell you why?'

'By all means,' said Jo.

'I am only a humble solicitor, as you know. But in my humble capacity I have had the inestimable privilege of supplying barristers with briefs. You may or may not know that briefs are as necessary for a barrister as water for a fish. Neither can survive without a sufficient and continuous supply of, in the one case, briefs, in the other, water. Perhaps you knew this already?'

'I had some idea of it,' said Jo.

'So you know, too, that the legal profession in this country is divided into two branches. The superior, that is the Bar; the lowly and inferior, that is the solicitor's profession. But, humble and lowly as we are, we do have the great honour of being allowed to supply the superior branch with their necessities of life, briefs. Naturally we count ourselves most blessed to be allowed to nourish such an admirable body of men and women as the Bar with their main source of existence. We do this from the moment the barrister is qualified. We help the young man, we bring distinction to the older man and, in a very large measure, we are responsible for the promotion to the Bench of the most distinguished members of the Bar. For you must know that judges are selected only from the Bar. You might have thought that, in the circumstances, there would be a measure of gratitude shown by the judge to the solicitor. Without his briefs, he would never have become a judge. Indeed, while he is still practising at the Bar, he usually treats solicitors not only with the utmost courtesy and consideration, but you might almost say that at times he shows actual signs of fawning on the hand that feeds him. You must forgive this rather long introduction.'

'Certainly,' said Jo, 'if it means that you want to help me.'

'I certainly do. And I will now tell you why. As soon as many of these courteous, polite barristers are elevated to the Bench their attitude towards their humble brethren, the solicitors, appears to undergo a marked change. "Where is the solicitor in the case?" they say. "How comes it that he has done so-and-so and not done so-and-so? While I am not trying an issue between him and his client as to whether he has been guilty of negligence, I feel bound to say that I can't see what answer he would have to such a claim." On another occasion he will go so far as to make the solicitor pay the costs personally, a horrible thing to do. In other words, he turns and bites the hand that fed him. All our loving care goes for nothing. Gone is the "Good morning, Mr Manage. How are you, my dear fellow? So glad to see you. Thank you so much for your instructions in the Wallaby case. They were, if I may say so, admirably drawn." Instead, we have: "It's outrageous that this notice wasn't given or this document not produced. What's a solicitor for?" When they ask that last question I always want to say, "To brief the barrister and that was once you, my Lord." But I don't. I should be sent to prison for contempt of Court. So I must be content with muttering to myself and telling my counsel to get up and stand up for me. Now, I think it was a charge of conspiracy you wanted to bring. That sounds admirable. I'd charge the whole lot of them with it, if I got the chance. But, of course, I must first be satisfied that you have a reasonable case. What's it all about?'

'Presumably you have read all about it, Mr Manage,' said Jo. 'Why shouldn't I sue Mr Justice Halliday and Mr Walsh for conspiracy to detain me against my will? The judge knew that by letting the police go I would be detained by Mr Walsh and he intended that I should be.'

'It's a nice idea,' said Mr Manage, 'a very nice idea indeed. My only regret is that I can't say that Mr Justice Halliday has ever made me pay the costs personally. Indeed, he has been rather an exception to the rule I was mentioning. However, that can't be helped. It should be an example to the others. Let me think.'

Mr Manage was silent for a short time. Then he said: 'As a mere solicitor, my opinion on a matter of this delicacy is of little value. We shall have to approach the superior branch. In other words, we shall need the opinion of counsel. Do you mind the expense?'

'Not if it will get me anywhere,' said Jo.

'Very well,' said Mr Manage. 'We will approach the most suitable of these learned gentlemen who is available. My first choice would be Mr Trent. He is quite intolerable, but so are most of them in their different ways, as a matter of fact. At the same time, he appears to me to know his law as well as any of them. Not that that means very much. The standard of lawyers at the Bar gets lower and lower.'

'Well, if the Bench is recruited from the Bar,' said Jo, 'you can't think much of the Bench.'

'I don't, Mrs Barnwell,' said Mr Manage. 'I don't. Between you and me there are only six decent lawyers in the country. Three are in the House of Lords, one's an ecclesiastical lawyer and the other two are dead. Mr Trent I consider to be the best of the extremely bad bunch which is available for your matter.'

'Then why don't you rely on your own opinion, Mr Manage?'

'That's quite simple, my dear Mrs Barnwell, quite simple. If I'm wrong, you could sue me. If I get counsel's opinion, you can't.'

'Even if he's careless?'

'Even, my dear Mrs Barnwell, if he is negligent to a degree which would justify the vituperative epithet of gross. The position is that, when your professional adviser, be he doctor, accountant, architect or humble solicitor, gives you the normal careless advice which the public have come to expect from him, you can take him to the Courts and his insurance company will pay you. But when the barrister is careless, far beyond the normal degree expected of him, you have no remedy against him and, of course, no remedy against the solicitor instructing him.'

'I must say it seems odd,' said Jo.

'It not only seems, but it is odd. I must make one qualification about my own position. If I took you now to a barrister who was a patent specialist and knew nothing about such things as judges conspiring with escaped convicts and, if he were foolish enough to accept the instructions and gave you advice which might have been admirable if you had just invented a machine for making the tea and shaving you at the same time, but which was completely off the rails in relation to a claim for false imprisonment, then indeed I might be liable to you for going to an obviously unsuitable man. I am taking no such risk in going to Mr Trent. That he is intolerable, I have already told you. That he may insult you, I add now, but he certainly practises in those courts where judges who conspire with escaped convicts would be brought, if such cases were in the normal run of things.'

'Very well,' said Jo. 'Let us go to Mr Trent.'

So a conference was arranged with Mr Trent's clerk and, at the appointed time, Jo and Mr Manage arrived at his chambers. They were not kept waiting.

'On the dot, you see, Mr Manage,' said Mr Trent cheerfully, as he welcomed them in. 'I see no reason why a barrister, however busy he may be, should not keep his appointments punctually. I expect you to be here on time. You have a right to expect that I am ready.'

'That is most kind,' said Jo.

'It is not intended to be,' said Mr Trent. 'It is intended to be good business. Members of the Bar don't like referring to the word "business." They consider that it lowers their prestige. In my view, nothing lowers a barrister's prestige except inefficiency. And I venture to think you will find none of that here, Mrs Barnwell. You see, I don't even pretend not to know your name. I have taken the trouble to memorise it. You will find no affectation here either.'

'What we hope to find,' said Jo, 'is the answer to my problem.'

'That goes without saying,' said Mr Trent. 'I have read these papers and come to a clear conclusion in the matter. That's something I deprecate in many of my colleagues. They give you so many alternatives in their opinions, so many "ifs" and "buts," that you don't know what they really are advising you. My advice may be wrong—it isn't, but, of course, you can't tell that—but it is always definite. The other day we won a case in the House of Lords. We had lost it before the judge of first instance. I had said that we should win it. "Should," mark you, not "would." I naturally cannot guarantee the correctness of every decision of a judge of first instance, even if I am appearing in the case. Some judges are so dense that you cannot penetrate their minds with any but the simplest propositions. I am not saying that was the case in the action I was telling you about. The judge was an excellent one, but unfortunately I was unable to accept the brief. The case was done by a very worthy and fairly able colleague, but, quite frankly, he wasn't up to it. So my client had to go to the Court of Appeal. There I would have appeared but, unfortunately, I was taken suddenly ill and had to return the brief. The case was lost again. You can imagine that at that stage my client must have been doubting the correctness of my advice. Four judges had now decided against my opinion. However, he came to consult me again and I advised him to go to the House of Lords. My advice was not that he "should" win there but that he "would" win. Provided, of course, that I was able to argue the case. I must say, my client took a lot of persuading to go on with the appeal. But, fortunately for him, in the end he agreed. I argued the case in the House of Lords and we won by a majority of three to two. The legal journals pointed out that that meant that six judges of high standing had decided in favour of my opponent and only three in favour of my client, and yet my client won. I pointed out, in a short and apt letter, that justice does not always go to the big battalions. I offer no apology for telling you all this. Mr Manage knows my reputation. That, no doubt, is why he comes to me. But you don't, Mrs Barnwell, and I always consider that the lay client— that is you, Mrs Barnwell—should get a fair idea of the man she is consulting.'

'I think you've given me an excellent idea,' said Jo. 'Apart, however, from what you have told me yourself, Mr Manage gave me a very good description of your qualities.'

'Did he?' said Mr Trent. 'He probably told you, then, that I was quite intolerable.'

Mr Manage blushed.

'So I am, Mrs Barnwell,' said Mr Trent, 'to most solicitors. Their abysmal ignorance and inefficiency is sometimes beyond bearing. I am not particularly referring to Mr Manage's firm, which is as good as any. Though, I am bound to say, that isn't anything much. Now, most members of the Bar don't talk like this, Mrs Barnwell. They flatter their clients, usually without the slightest justification. You will gather that I don't. I tell them exactly what I think of them, and I am bound to admit that some of them don't come back for more. Indeed, if it were not for the fact that fortunately nature had endowed me with certain qualities which peculiarly suit me for this profession—I claim no credit for it, any more than one claims credit for having been born—if it were not for that fact, I don't suppose I should have a single client. I should have had to give up the Bar years ago. Fortunately, as you can see from the briefs on the table, that lamentable event did not occur. Solicitors have to come to me, whether they like it or not. I don't suppose Mr Manage likes it any better than most of the others. Now, shall we proceed?'

'Yes, please,' said Jo.

'You want to know whether you would have a reasonable chance of succeeding in an action for conspiracy against Mr Justice Halliday and Mr Walsh, the conspiracy being to imprison you falsely. The answer to that question is, quite simply, yes. If the action were tried by a judge, he would, in my view, if the case were properly argued in front of him, be bound to find in your favour.

If the case came before a jury, I cannot predict with the same certainty what they would say. But, even if they decided against you, you would have a fair chance of upsetting their verdict on appeal.'

'Well, that's very good hearing,' said Jo. 'We'll start at once.'

'Wait a moment,' said Mr Trent. 'The two questions which would arise in your action are whether the claim is legally justified and, secondly, what are the damages. If, as I think it would be, the first question is decided in your favour, the second question arises. What are the damages? Now normally they might be heavy. But I am bound to say that, in the very peculiar and exceptional circumstances of this case, I think you would be lucky if you were awarded more than £5. That amount the defendant would certainly pay into court and, if you recovered no more, you would have the pleasure of paying the costs of both sides. Of course, you could accept the £5, but I rather think that would not appeal to you.'

'£5!' said Jo indignantly. 'Can decent citizens be imprisoned by judges without justification and only recover £5?'

'No,' said Mr Trent, 'I didn't say that. But I feel quite sure that any judge or jury would hold that you were not a decent citizen, and that you were only detained in order that a wrong for which you were responsible could be remedied.'

'Are you on their side or mine?' asked Jo.

'I am on no one's side yet,' said Mr Trent. 'I am advising you to the best of my ability, which, as I have already indicated to you, is considerable. In the light of the Tribunal's report, any judge or jury would take the view that Mr Walsh was wrongly convicted and that you were in all probability responsible for that conviction.'

'He's a murderer,' said Jo. 'He murdered my husband.'

'Fortunately,' said Mr Trent, 'what you say to me is

privileged and will, of course, be treated by me in complete confidence, but, if you are wise, you won't make statements like that outside these chambers.'

'That is where I am going anyway,' said Jo, 'and I shall say and do what I please there,' and she left the room abruptly.

'I'm sorry,' said Mr Manage to Mr Trent, 'but she feels strongly on the subject.'

'It is quite unnecessary to apologise,' said Mr Trent. 'I have only proved you to be right—in your advice to your client about me, I mean.'

'It's nice to be right for once,' said Mr Manage.

'I hope you won't have to wait too long for the next time,' said Mr Trent.

CHAPTER NINETEEN

All Square

MILES HAMPTON never had his interview on television. The best he could get was a ghosted article in one of the Sunday newspapers. It was called: 'Why I Refused To Give Evidence,' and Miles received £100 for being a party to it. He read the article he was supposed to have written, and, though he could not fully understand the reasons, as stated, why he had not given evidence, he enjoyed seeing his name and photograph in the paper. He enjoyed the £100 almost as much. And, in the circumstances, he considered that, all in all, he had not done so badly. Instead of receiving anything up to seven years for perjury he had had an interesting experience, received a good deal of publicity and been paid for it.

Mrs Meadowes duly married her new husband and both of them were good value, in the public houses which they frequented, for some months.

Herbert Adams went back to his bench in the park and waited for something else to happen.

Mr Allwinter went back to his art and had several ideas for pictures which he put into execution. One, a large canvas, called 'Mr Justice Halliday at home' and showing accurately the scene at the judge's house during the enquiry, was shown in the Academy. The judge bought it quickly. Mr Allwinter began another.

Angela and Charles began to see more and more of each other, with Lonsdale's entire approval.

Lonsdale himself, after taking a short rest, began to consider fresh financial ventures. About six weeks after his release he was taking, as he often did, a stroll in the evening near his London house when a large blue car ran into and over him in the middle of the road. He was fatally injured, though not killed on the spot. The car endeavoured to drive on, but somehow the collision had affected the steering and it swerved into a lamp-post. In the result, the police, who were quickly on the scene, were able to take a statement from the driver, after Lonsdale had been rushed to hospital. There were no independent witnesses but the driver explained that the injured man had suddenly rushed into the middle of the road in front of the car, giving it no chance. The police might have had no difficulty in accepting this statement as true, but for the fact that the driver was Jo Barnwell.

As soon as they discovered her identity, they did all they could to get a statement from Lonsdale before he died. A policeman sat by his bed the whole time, night and day.

It was obvious that he would die, but a day after the accident he recovered consciousness sufficiently to speak. He was asked how the accident happened. Before he answered the question, he asked:

'Did the driver stop?'

He was told that she couldn't help it.

'Then you know who she is?' he asked.

'Yes,' said the police officer.

'What was her version?' asked Lonsdale.

The officer told him.

'Absolutely correct,' said Lonsdale, and closed his eyes.

'Nurse,' called the officer. 'Quick. He's gone almost purple.'

Later, recovering consciousness again for the last time, he asked to see Jo alone. She knew by then that he had confirmed her story.

'Why did you tell a lie?' she asked. 'You know I did it on purpose.'

'I know,' he said, 'but I've a great regard for you, Jo, and I didn't mind that sort of attack. That was quite straightforward. I ought to have thought you might try it. After all, it's only what I did to Adolphus myself.'

'Then it was you, and you managed to lie about that too.'

'I didn't, Jo. I didn't have to, though I would have, if necessary.'

'You must have told your daughter you were innocent. I'm sure she said you had.'

'I only told her and everyone else that I'd been convicted by perjury. That was true enough.'

'So the only lie you've ever told was to save me?'

'Yes, Jo. I'm not sure that you deserve it. Fancy suggesting that I'd let anyone else run over Adolphus for me. He'd have been sure to make a mess of it. But I did better than you, Jo. I killed him outright.'

'I did try, darling,' said Jo apologetically.